I0777845

Reservation

Book Five of The Gifted Series

Ana Ban

FIVE POINT PUBLISHING

Five Point Publishing

www.fivepointpublishing.com

Although every precaution has been taken to verify the accuracy of the information contained herein, the author and publisher assume no responsibility for any errors or omissions. No liability is assumed for damages that may result from the use of information contained within.

All Persons Fictitious Disclaimer:

This book is a work of fiction. Any similarity between the characters and situations within its pages and places or persons, living or dead, is unintentional and coincidental.

ISBN 978-1-959716-13-6 (Paperback)

[1.Fantasy 2.Romance]

First Edition

Printed in the USA

This book is dedicated to my aunt,
Deb Kofal.
Your endless energy and caring spirit never cease to amaze me.
Thank you for always supporting my endeavours.

Contents

For a full family tree, please visit
www.anabannovels.com/giftedtree

Chapter 1

Sipping on the strong caffeine-laced drink, I perused the classifieds and did my best to ignore the mopey man across from me. The sun shone brightly outside the small café, heating the air and the dry, cracked earth to equal levels of sweltering. Though a far cry from the wilds of Wisconsin, New Mexico had a certain familiarity I couldn't overlook.

Circling another option for work, I looked up and rolled my eyes when I realized my companion had become distracted. "You need to look for work, too."

The man with soft brown eyes turned his attention away from the scantily clad girls across the room and focused back on me. "Why? It's not like we're going to stay long."

Closing my eyes, I took in a steadying breath before answering. "Frances, you remember the deal you made with Talon."

With a grunt, he spun the paper around to see what I'd already circled. "Boring, boring, boring. Come on, Lani, let's do something fun."

"Find *something*," I said, at the end of my patience. "And then we can explore."

He slouched into his seat, disgruntled but still looking through the classifieds. The day I'd agreed to babysit this formerly evil creature was one I'd come to regret.

Every. Single. Day.

Jade and Talon—my closest friend and her mate—were supposed to meet up with me sooner than this but had come across trouble of their own. I couldn't begrudge them helping out family, but if Frances made it through another day without me ripping his head off, I would be the most surprised of all.

Draining my mug, I decided another was in order to make it through the day. Approaching the counter for a refill, I tuned in to the conversations around me.

Las Cruces seemed to be a bustling city, filled with locally owned shops and delicious restaurants. The Mescalero Apache Tribe—our main reason for traveling to the southwest—was a little over an hour away. We'd stopped in Las Cruces since there seemed to be more opportunity for work.

Even though money wasn't so much an issue, working would help to ingratiate ourselves into society. Being a contributing member of society had also been part of Frances' penalty. Besides, a measly hundred miles was nothing when you possessed supernatural speed.

My ears picked up a particularly frustrated man spewing whispered curses at his phone. While I preferred the outdoors, technology had always fascinated me. With oodles of time and no family or friends to speak of, I'd had ample opportunity to learn.

It also helped to see technological progress first-hand.

Turning with my filled mug in my hands, I spied the man—his deep brown skin creased from age and too many hours in the sun—just a table over. Wanting to put him out of his misery, I wandered over and spoke softly so as to not frighten him. "Sounds like that thing is getting the best of you."

"Smartphone, my left toe. There's nothing smart about them!"

With a smile, I placed a hand on the back of the empty chair. "May I?"

"Please," he said, blowing out a breath. "You young people are always so much better with this stuff."

Grinning privately at his misinterpretation of my existence, I sat and grasped the phone lightly in one palm. "What are you trying to do?"

"Access my e-mail. Nothing I do seems to work." Entering the settings, I took a quick perusal, touched a few buttons, and asked him to type in his password. When he did, his mail popped in. His jaw dropped open, staring at the small device in bafflement. "Now, how in the world did you do that?"

"Oh, you know, magic," I said with a wink.

"I owe you a coffee. Emanuel Hernandez, you are?" he said, offering his hand.

"Lani Brown," I told him, using the name currently on my license and accepting the friendly gesture.

"If there's anything I can do to repay you, Lani, please tell me. How about that coffee?"

I laughed and shook my head. "No, but thank you. My...cousin and I"—here I paused, taking the opportunity to gesture in Frances' direction—"are new in town and need to get on the job hunt."

"You're hired," he blurted out.

It was my turn to drop my jaw. "What do you mean?"

"I mean, I run a small construction company out of Tularosa. My office manager just quit, and if you're interested in driving that far, you're hired." Words escaped me. How very convenient. Tularosa was only twenty minutes from the reservation, a much easier jaunt than Las Cruces would be.

"That sounds perfect. You wouldn't happen to need a laborer, would you?" We both looked over at Frances, who was slowly banging his head against the table. I stifled a laugh at his predicament and turned back to the man beside me. "He's...stronger than he looks."

"I could use another laborer," Emanuel said, studying Frances. "He have any experience?"

"Not really. But he's a hard worker and a fast learner."

Emanuel nodded. "If you're willing to vouch for him, I'll give him a test run. How much experience do you need to shovel dirt, anyway?"

"Indeed. When would you need us to begin?"

He shrugged and checked the time on his phone. "I'm headed to the office now. Are you free?"

Nodding, I thanked Emanuel profusely before making my way back to Frances. "I've solved our problems. Let's go."

Grabbing my bag and slinging it across my shoulders, I waited for Frances to catch up. "What do you mean?"

"I got us both jobs. We're meeting with him now."

Suspicion clouded his eyes. "What, exactly, will I be doing?"

Walking to the exit, I answered, "You'll be outside."

"And?"

"And working with the earth."

"Lani...."

"How does construction sound to you?" I asked, refusing to meet his gaze.

"You want me to perform...manual labor?" Frances sounded incredulous, pausing beside the passenger side of the second-hand truck I'd purchased for this journey.

"It's something new, exciting. Isn't that what you wanted?" Slipping into the driver's side, I missed his grumbled remark. It didn't matter to me whether Frances was happy with his new position. He still had a lot to atone for, and his only alternative was a locked cell.

I was willing to give him a second chance, per Jade's wishes, but that didn't mean I would slack in my duties.

While Frances sulked beside me, I steered the truck away from the city and toward Tularosa. There were still a lot of wide-open spaces in this part of the state, and I found the expanse of sand soothing. An unusual beauty could be found in the scraggy cliffs and lone cacti standing firm against the sun and wind.

It was a land of survivors. I could appreciate that.

As we drove, we came upon White Sands National Park, a gorgeous stretch of—as the name aptly suggests—white sand. The dunes were eerily similar to the deserts of the Middle East and had been used by Hollywood in several movies because of it.

"I'll give New Mexico this: there are definitely some hidden gems here," Frances said, sitting straight now and watching out the window as we passed the pristine land.

"It certainly has its own beauty. Are you done being mad at me now?"

"I'm reserving judgment until after my first day." Frances slouched, sulking again. I sighed.

Jade and Talon couldn't get here fast enough.

∞ ∞ ∞

EMANUEL BEAT US TO THE office by minutes, and I took a good look around as we parked. The office was no more than a trailer, set on a patch of desert and surrounded by construction equipment. Emanuel waited at the door, so we wasted no time in joining him.

"Nice to meet you," Emanuel said, offering his hand to Frances. "What's your name?"

"Frances Borg," he answered proudly. Behind my back, I crossed my fingers that he would behave himself.

"Come on in," Emanuel said, opening the door and gesturing us through.

There were four desks inside, two pushed together on each side of the room. File cabinets were scattered along the walls, and stale coffee sat in a pot on top of a mini fridge. One man sat behind a desk, barely visible behind the stacks of paperwork. He looked frazzled but smiled on seeing us. "Hey, Manny. Who's this?"

"Dave, this is Lani, our new office gal, and Frances. We're going to test him out in the field."

Dave looked Frances up and down with a smirk. "Good luck."

Frances seemed put off by this, and I looked over at him to see what these men saw. Though he was traditionally handsome, with dark features and a lean build, he definitely wasn't my type—especially not with the personality that came with those looks.

What the two other men in the room probably saw was the smooth skin and soft hands—a dead giveaway to the fact that Frances had never performed manual labor in his life. Crossing his arms, Frances pouted. "I'll be the best laborer you've ever had."

He very well could be, with the right motivation. If his petulant teenager attitude would get him to work hard just to prove these men wrong, I'd take it. Shaking Dave's hand, I said, "Nice to meet you. What do you do here?"

"I'm the estimator, but we've been without an office person for the last week, so I've had to help out with payroll and some other things that I really shouldn't be in charge of."

Laughing lightly, I looked back to Emanuel. "What all do you need me to do?"

"Payroll, receivables, payables—and anything else that might come up. Tell you what, I'll bring Frances over to the job site to get him started and let you get acquainted with Dave, then I'll be back."

"Sounds good."

"Uh, Manny? Frances needs to fill out some paperwork first," Dave reminded him.

"Oh, of course. Just a few papers, Frances. You too, Lani," Emanuel said with a sheepish grin. Nodding, I accepted the small packet from Dave and began filling it out. Frances made himself comfortable at one of the desks, and we completed the paperwork in silence. Emanuel disappeared for a few minutes, returning as we wrapped up. He held out a pair of boots to Frances. "You'll need steel-toed. These should work for a day. Also, got you a hard hat and vest."

"Orange," Frances said with no small amount of horror, grasping the material between two fingers. "Lovely."

"Makes you easier to see, so the big equipment won't crush you," Emanuel said with a chuckle. "Come on, I'll drive you over."

Frances sent me a death glare as he left, which I subsequently ignored. Dave watched them go, then said, "He doesn't seem too happy about being here."

"He'll be fine. Where can I start?"

Dave showed me my desk—one of the two on the opposite side of the room from his—and gave me a brief rundown on the filing system. The first thing I set to work on was organizing the momentous piles of paper into like stacks, then booted up the ancient computer to see what kind of software they were using. After getting a feel for their system, I began with the easiest task—entering payables. It would also get rid of one of the largest piles of paper.

Once Emanuel came back, he showed me their job numbering system and daily paperwork that would be turned in from the foremen in the field. "Seems simple enough. Once I get all this cleared up, we'll talk about some organizational changes."

"Whatever works for you." Emanuel gave an easy shrug. "And as long as it doesn't add much more work for any of us, you'll have free rein."

"What will my hours be?"

"Seven-thirty to four, Monday through Friday. If you need more time to get anything done, just let me know. We're pretty flexible."

"Sounds good," I said before getting back to work.

By the end of the day, I'd gotten a decent handle on the mess that had been my desk and had some ideas to streamline the whole process. As we got ready to leave for the day, Emanuel offered to show me the way to the job site so I could pick up Frances. We would have to look into getting him his own car, as he would likely have different hours than I did—and him running to work would look suspicious.

I followed Emanuel in the truck into the mountainous area of the reservation. It was a beautiful land, and I found myself watching the scenery out the window more than the road. Taking advantage of the drive, I decided to give Jade a call and update her on our progress and find out hers. When she picked up, I got right to the point. "Jade, where are you?"

"We're just outside San Francisco," she said. "How is everything? Where are you?"

"We stopped in Las Cruces, and I found us work. Jade, you need to come soon. I'm going to strangle him."

"Sorry, Lani, I don't have great reception; you must be cutting out."

"Jade Callaghan, don't you dare," I told her sternly. "You can hear me fine."

"You're right, I can. We—uh, well, we had some setbacks, but we should be there no later than next week."

"Is this woman in danger? Do we need to go to her now?"

I paused, not recognizing the deep, slightly accented voice that had come over the line. "Jade? Who was that?"

"His name is Lucius. It's a long story, but we've added a few members to our group."

"All right then," I said slowly. "Thank you for your concern, Lucius, but I can handle myself. If Jade would like Frances to make it past this week, she'll have to come deal with him herself."

"We'll be there soon, Lani, I promise," Jade assured me. "What job did you get?"

"An office position at a construction firm. Frances will be a...laborer," I said, allowing my amusement to bubble over. "He's livid."

"It'll be good for him," Jade said. After a brief pause, she continued, "Hang on a sec, I'm going to take you off speaker."

I waited for her to move away from the noise of people, knowing she had a story to tell me. My curiosity was bubbling over—

they were already dealing with an unknown Elemental with memory loss; what else had they come across?

"We were captured by shadowmen," Jade said after a minute. It was much quieter on her end, so I imagined she'd moved well away from the group.

"What!" I practically screeched. Then, I realized I was speaking to her on the phone, so she was obviously all right. Calmer, I asked, "What happened?"

"Three shadowmen locked up the four of us. But, Lani, get this—Kate saved us. She's incredibly powerful, even more than me. She actually healed their souls."

My jaw worked, but no sound came out. I'd never heard of this before. "That is amazing. And these shadowmen—Lucius is one of them?"

"Yes. Lucius, Silas, and Augustus. They'd led rather extraordinary lives, at least until the darkness took hold."

I could hear the empathy Jade felt for these men and knew her gift must be in overdrive. "You can trust them?"

"I believe so, yes. Talon took their blood, just like he did with Frances, so he could keep track of them if need be. They also agreed to show me some of their spells—they have such a wealth of knowledge between them. And I'm working on a theory about how Frances seems...younger, and these three do not. I think it's because of when they began to turn to the darkness."

"Interesting theory. So long as you're safe, that's all that matters." Hitting the city limits of the reservation, I told Jade I would call to update her again in a few days.

Outside the small town, Emanuel pulled up to a gatehouse, where he spoke to a guard for a few moments before we both got waved through. Frances had been put to work on a copper mine, which turned out to be wildly different than what I'd imagined. There were no dwarves with pickaxes whistling as they worked in underground caves. Instead, the fenced-off area consisted of a wide expanse of land with dirt roads spiraling down into a deep pit. Huge trucks hunkered along, and I was shocked to realize one tire on the humongous vehicle was larger than my whole truck.

Emanuel pulled to a stop before entering the actual work zone, and I followed suit. I got out and walked up to him, accepting the hard hat and vest as he began pointing out different aspects of the mine and what his crew worked on.

"Frances is over there," he said, motioning to the far side of the chasm.

The crew looked like ants against the red earth, though with my enhanced vision, I could pick out Frances easily. Unhooking a walkie-talkie from his belt, Emanuel spoke into it, letting his foreman know to release Frances for the day.

He veered off the main group and made his way over to us. When I focused on his features, to my surprise, Frances had a grin on his face. As he neared us, the smile faded into his usual sulking look, but I knew the truth.

"How was your first day?"

"Fine," he mumbled.

"Juan was impressed by you," Emanuel said, and Frances' face brightened instantly.

"Really?" He looked over at me again, wiping the smile from his face. When he continued, he suddenly looked the epitome of nonchalant. "That's cool."

Emanuel and I shared a look, and I pressed my lips together to keep from laughing. "Ready to go?"

"Sure."

"Thank you again," I said to Emanuel. "We owe you."

He opened his mouth to respond, but sudden shouts had us all turning back toward the crew on the other side of the mine. We watched, frozen in horror, as part of the road began to collapse, and a piece of equipment began to fall.

It started to tip sideways, and I watched as if in slow motion, hesitating only briefly. One moment, I stood beside Emanuel and Frances; the next, I was a blur of motion, racing to the catastrophe in progress.

As I ran, I took in several things at once: the terrified operator in the toppling excavator, the rockslide closing in on a crew further down the chasm, and another man racing toward the scene to help. My eyes flicked over the running man for only an instant, but I felt something shift inside me at the brief contact. Ignoring it, I put my focus on the machine.

Mother Earth, strong and true. Halt your tremble, make it firm. Save the lives of your children; this I ask of you.

Sending the power of my words through the earth, the mine shook with the effort of holding the falling rock and sand in place. When I reached the machine, it took everything in me to hold it there, hovering on the edge.

Realizing I couldn't rescue the operator inside while concentrating so wholly on keeping the machine in place, it was a relief to see Frances appear above, reaching into the cab to pull the operator out.

The crew below me had scattered, so once I let go, the machine could tumble to the ground without any casualties. I released my hold and watched as it began to fall.

Everything happened so quickly, the lone man running to the rescue was still on a forward trajectory—and on a direct path with the crumbling section of earth caused by the falling excavator. Launching myself at the heroic man, I tackled him to the ground as the equipment made an impact with the bottom. We rolled to a stop as a large cloud of sand and debris shot into the air like a geyser.

Automatically, I covered the head of the man I'd found myself sprawled across, knowing even if I did get hit that I would heal quickly.

Strangely terrified that this man would be injured, I smothered him with my own head and arms. I knew, deep down, I would do anything to protect him.

Once the major debris landed and the dust began to slowly trickle back down to earth, I raised my head to look into the eyes of the man I'd saved. He stared back at me, the deep chocolate brown irises gazing into my very soul. Something stirred inside me in recognition, something I knew I would fight tooth and nail.

This man was my mate.

Chapter 2

We stared at each other for several long moments; I got sucked into his dark gaze, my mind fighting against my baser instincts. Finally, shouts and other noises intruded on our moment, and I pushed myself off the man with a start.

"You didn't see me," I said emphatically, conveying my urgency with a look, my power glowing in my eyes. "Got it?"

Though baffled, he still nodded his agreement to my odd request. Still, I found myself hesitating, torn between survival and some unnamed emotion that was brand new and overwhelming. With something akin to a growl, I turned and disappeared.

I knew I would have a lot of explaining to do, but for now, if I could limit the number of people who questioned how I could have gotten from one side of the mine to the other in a split second down to one, I would take it.

In a matter of moments, I was back at my truck, and I took a few more to make myself presentable. Brushing out most of the debris from my hair, I realized I couldn't do much about my outfit or the smudges on my skin. Maybe I would just tell everyone I fell down.

I took off at a jog to catch up with Emanuel, who was still hurrying to the accident site. When he saw me at his side, he asked, "Did you notify the guard?"

Frances must have given us a cover story before he'd run over to help. "Yes. Is everyone okay?"

"We'll find out," he replied, worry marring his tone. When we made it to the other side, we found Emanuel's crew in a huddle around Frances, staring down at the devastation the excavator had wreaked.

"Everyone is okay," the foreman—who I guessed was Juan, based on what Emanuel had said earlier—told us, gesturing with his walkie-talkie to encompass the other crews, as well.

The man I'd saved—my mate—stood at the back, gaze steady on me. There wasn't as much confusion or shock as I would have expected from what had just happened, but maybe he had hit his head.

Emanuel looked to the operator and asked, "How did you get out of there?"

"Frances pulled me out," the man replied, slapping Frances on the back. "He saved my life."

Frances looked pleased with himself but also startled by the sudden attention. I had a feeling he hadn't gotten a lot of praise in his life as a shadowman, or perhaps even before. Feeling eyes boring into me, I looked away from Frances and back to the man that I had no idea how to handle.

Just a year ago, I'd been constantly on the run, avoiding relationships of all varieties. Because of Jade—and, by extension, Talon—I'd slowly come to realize that not all men were inherently evil. Even Frances, who had given up his soul at such a young age, still had enough good in him to be saved. And now, he helped to rescue humans when he easily could have held back.

My gaze went back to the man who would be my mate, and I felt pity for him. Not because of who he was but because of who *I* was. I could never give him what he needed, what he deserved. A girl with no past and an inherent fear of relationships could not be a worthy mate.

The sorrow I felt must have been plain on my face, for his eyebrows drew together in confusion. For a moment, I considered reaching out to him to reassure him there was nothing wrong with him, but establishing a telepathic link now would only complicate matters more.

Sighing, I turned and began to walk back to my truck. It would be a while before Frances would be able to leave—an accident like this would need to be investigated—and I would wait for him there.

When I reached the area where I'd parked, I started to pull the handle when I heard a voice calling out to me. "Hey, wait up!"

Closing my eyes for just a moment, I took a deep breath before turning to face my destiny. "Yes?"

The man with broad shoulders and a lean frame paused just a few feet away, seeming hesitant by my cold response. "I—I just wanted to thank you."

"You're welcome," I said shortly, turning again to climb into the truck. His hand grabbed the door before I could close it, and his body was suddenly in my space. Sucking in a breath, I met his eyes again. A chunk of his long hair had escaped from its clasp to fall across his shoulder. I had the sudden urge to touch the silky tendril, to curl it around my fingers like mist wrapping around a tree. Fear of my wayward thoughts put more venom in my tone than I meant. "What do you want?"

"Your name," he replied easily.

My lips pressed into a thin line, but I answered him anyway. "Lani."

"I'm Samson," he said, holding out his hand. I stared at it until he pulled it back. "Okay, then. Not the touchy-feely type, that's cool. Of course, a handshake is nothing compared to laying on top of me, is it?"

I choked out a laugh at his audacity, but I knew I had to nip this in the bud before he could get carried away. "I'm glad you're okay, but this can't happen."

"What can't happen?" he asked, cocking his head to the side.

Gesturing between us, I said, "This."

He caught my hand mid-air, grasping it lightly to examine it. "Such a delicate hand, yet so powerful."

I pulled my hand back with a snap and glared at him. "I'm not a delicate flower."

His lips tipped up in the corner, a sexy, crooked smile that sent my pulse racing. "Funny, as your name means flower."

"How could you possibly know that?"

Samson leaned close until I could feel his breath on my face. It felt warm, inviting. His blood pumped through the vein in his neck, beckoning me closer. Just a taste, it whispered. I could smell the underlying sweet scent of creosote on his skin, and my tongue darted out to moisten my suddenly parched lips.

"I know more than you'd believe," he said softly. "Have dinner with me."

"What?" I asked, snapping back to reality. "No."

"Tonight would work. Or tomorrow, anytime. It's the weekend, after all."

"What part of 'no' do you not understand?"

"I guess all of it. So, what do you say? Dinner tonight or tomorrow?"

"I"—my mouth hung open, unable to keep up with his easy attitude—"I have other things to do."

"Like what?"

"Finding a place to live."

"My uncle is renting a house. It's two bedrooms, so it'll work for you and your cousin. Done. What else?"

My jaw worked as I was left speechless. My cousin? Right— that's what I'd called Frances. Clearly defeated, I still mumbled, "It's not that easy."

"Sure it is. I'll take you there as soon as we wrap up here. It's move-in ready and right in town, so you won't be far from the office, and Frances won't be far from the job site."

"Are you seriously not going to ask me how I came to save you?"

His eyes twinkled back at me, a wealth of emotion and surprising depth of intelligence in the dark pools. My breath hitched in my throat. "You'll tell me when you're ready. Not to worry, your secret is safe with me."

And for a moment, I believed him. I looked away and spotted Frances heading our way. "MSHA will be here Monday. We'll have to answer more questions then, but Manny told us to take off. What's up, Samson?"

"I've got a place for you to live," Samson said. "We can go there now."

"Cool." Frances shrugged and hopped into the bed of the truck. "I'll ride back here."

Samson sent me a huge, triumphant grin before walking around to the passenger door and sliding in. "Let's go."

Somehow, I'd just been bamboozled by a former shadowman and my mate. When had this become my life? Starting the engine, I let out a huff of air. "Fine, but only because we need somewhere to live."

With a smug grin, Samson crossed his arms over his chest and leaned back in the seat. "Go left after you leave the gate."

Following his directions, we came to a stop in front of a small, single-level home on a square piece of property. There were rose bushes in front and the typical rock landscape otherwise. Samson had called his uncle to meet us but got out and dug a spare key from under a fake rock.

"Home sweet home," he said, allowing Frances and me to enter first.

I stepped inside hesitantly, still reeling from the strange turn of events. Though I had to dissuade Samson from any notion of a relationship, I was also waiting for the bomb to drop. Either him freaking out about what had happened or him telling others—or both.

Worst case scenario, I could brainwash him, much like Frances had done with Emanuel, to make him think I'd gone to the guard and that Frances hadn't joined us yet before the accident happened. I was sure he'd done something similar with the crew, but he probably had left Samson alone, as we both could tell he was Gifted. Frances didn't know yet about our other connection, and I hoped to avoid that particular topic.

We walked into a small living room with a kitchen directly behind it. There were bedrooms on either end of the home, with bathrooms next to each. It would be perfect for however long Frances and I needed to stay.

"It's great," I said with a defeated sigh.

"Told you. Now, how about that dinner?"

Saved from answering by the entrance of an older man, I turned to introduce myself. He had dark hair, long and tied at the base of his neck with a leather cord. He reminded me of Talon in that aspect.

"Hi there," he said in a deep, velvety voice. "I'm Viktor, Samson's uncle. Nice to meet you."

"Lani," I said, accepting his hand to shake. His skin felt warm, and I felt a familiar tingle that alerted me to the fact that this man was also Gifted. "It's a beautiful home."

"It'll do," he responded casually. Frances came out of one of the rooms and introduced himself. "Just the two of you?"

"Yes," I said. "We're cousins."

Viktor nodded. "We're pretty relaxed about things here. If you want the place, I'll need first and last month's rent. If Samson will vouch for you, I won't need to do a background check."

"I'll vouch for them," Samson said, that same twinkle in his eye.

"How soon can we move in?"

"Now, if you'd like. You have any stuff?"

"Not yet," I said with half a smile.

Viktor and Samson exchanged a look, then came upon some kind of silent, mutual agreement. "There're some kitchen basics already in the cupboards, and we can set you up with a couple of beds," Samson said. "There's a thrift store in town; you can find any other furniture you need pretty reasonably."

"That would be great."

"Samson and I will go get the beds," his uncle said. "We'll be back in an hour or less."

Nodding, I looked over to Frances, who seemed to be brimming with questions. Once the two men left, he asked the most pertinent one—the one I'd been trying to avoid. "He's your mate, isn't he?"

For several beats, I stared at Frances, debating whether to bite his head off or ignore him. To keep the peace, I chose the latter— though the brief fantasy of strangling him lifted my spirits.

"Let's go to the thrift store. We'll pick up a couple pieces of furniture." Without waiting for his reply, I marched out the door, locking it and replacing the key under the fake rock once he'd joined me outside. When we were underway, I continued, "I've got enough cash to cover the rent, but this way, we can pretend we went to the bank. Most people don't walk around with that kind of money. Don't want to look suspicious."

"I didn't influence his mind, so I'm pretty sure you already look suspicious."

Sending him a glare, my look softened after a moment's thought. "Thank you for your help earlier. And your quick thinking."

"I haven't taken over a mind since...." He trailed off, but we both knew he was talking about his shadowman life.

"It was for a good cause. Just don't get in the habit." We were silent for most of the drive when something Jade had told me earlier came to mind. "Jade and her cousin saved three more shadowmen."

"Really?" he asked, sitting up straight. "Wait, what can her cousin do?"

"Apparently, she healed their souls. Different than what Jade did with you, but same result."

Frances sat back again, thinking this through. "Interesting."

"She also mentioned they are teaching her some of their spells." He remained silent, though I could tell I had his full attention. "Well, I was wondering—when we have time—if you would show me some things."

"Are you admitting I know things you don't?"

With a groan, I shook my head. "Never mind. Forget I asked."

"Aw, come on, Lani. It'll be fun."

"You'd be willing?" I asked, glancing over at him again.

Though he acted like a sulky teen most of the time, I had to remember that he was, in fact, a very powerful creature. Perhaps it was time I started treating him as such. He shrugged with practiced insouciance. "Sure. It could be cool."

Not wanting to add a biting remark, I pulled along the curb of the thrift store and got out. It wasn't a huge store by any means, but I was surprised by the number of items crammed into the space when we entered.

"Hi there!" said a cheerful voice from behind a towering pile of pillows. "How can I help you?"

Moving around the crowded space until I could see the face that matched the voice, I smiled warmly at the young woman, who grinned brightly back at me. Sensing the same kind of connection to her that I got with all Gifted, I felt my way slowly. "Hi, we're just looking for a few things for a house."

Huge, dark eyes lit up at the news. "Oh, newcomers! My favorite. I'm Nova, what's your name?"

"Lani," I replied, then gestured toward Frances. "This is my cousin, Frances."

"Well, aren't you a handsome thing?" Nova approached Frances and looped a hand through his arm. "Tell me all about the house. Did you buy or rent?"

"Rent," I said with amusement.

"That must be Uncle Vik's place."

"Viktor is your uncle?" I asked, suddenly feeling trapped.

"Not by blood. My mom's sister is married to his brother, so we treat each other like family."

Trying to work out the family tree, I asked, "Do you know Samson, then?"

"Of course, he's my cousin. For real cousin, not like with Vik."

Related to Samson and Gifted. We seemed to have hit the jackpot with this town. Frances spoke up. "I'm working with Samson at the mine."

Nova pulled away, eyeing Frances up and down. "Really? But you're so pretty. Pretty boys don't work construction."

Frances grinned over at me. "I like her."

Rolling my eyes, I looked back to Nova. "What do you have for living room furniture?"

We ended up with two comfortable chairs with a faded floral print in lieu of a couch and two nightstands. There was also a small dining table that Nova promised to hold until the next day when we could come back and pick it up.

With our new furnishings, we headed back to the rental house to find Viktor and Samson had just arrived with two mattresses in the back of Viktor's truck.

Frances hurried out to help them, and I hung back, easily lifting one of the nightstands but leaving the larger pieces for the men. This was always the difficult part of being around humans—hiding my strength to keep up appearances.

The men brought all the furniture inside, and I rearranged it as I saw necessary. I handed the first and last month's rent over to Viktor, and Frances led him outside, leaving Samson with me. Something strange and frightening rose up from my stomach to my chest. Nerves. "Thank you for your help."

"Anytime," he said, offering his easy smile. "So, about dinner tomorrow—"

"Samson, I can't. I just—I can't."

He stepped close. Automatically, I took a step back. His scent overwhelmed me anyway. My breath came out in short, quick little gasps. What was happening to me? I'd never had any kind of physical reaction to a man before. This was new and unnerving. It had to stop.

"You can, Lani. And you should—but I won't force you." Samson reached out and tucked a lock of hair behind my ear. Lightning crackled from that point and raced through my blood. "I also won't give up."

With that, he took a step back. I felt equal parts relief and anguish. "Samson."

He turned back, his dark gaze meeting mine. "Lani."

"I wish you would," I said. I had to be honest as much as I could. "Give up, I mean. It would be for the best."

"The best for you or for me?"

"Both."

He watched me quietly, studied each line and plane of my face. Then, with his signature grin, he shrugged. "Too bad."

Frances and I spent the evening unpacking, such as it were. We'd need to acquire a special fridge to store blood, but otherwise, we didn't need much. Most of what we had was for appearance's sake only.

I did place candles around the house, with the largest concentration in my room. Call me old-fashioned, but I preferred to relax by candlelight instead of electricity. We also placed protection around the house and grounds—though we didn't expect any trouble, it had a tendency to find me.

As evening turned to night, Frances and I set out to find a spot to practice. We went deep into the desert, skirting around the base of a hill to the north and finding a decent stretch of flat land, well hidden from the town. Frances walked the perimeter of our new training area slowly, getting a sense for it.

"Do you feel that?" I asked, staring further north.

Frances looked up and put his hands out as if searching for something out of the ordinary. "No, nothing. What is it?"

"I'm not sure." Frowning, I searched the area. "Whatever it is, it's not hostile. More like...like a sacred space."

"We're not in it, are we?"

"No, but—it feels as if it's calling to me."

"Want to go check it out?"

A few moments more, I stared, opening myself up. "No. Not yet. I'm not meant to go yet."

Frances didn't question this, he merely completed his scouting circle. Glancing up at me, he asked, "So, is there anything in particular you'd like to learn?"

"I'm not sure."

"Why don't we start with something simple? Have you ever fashioned clothing for yourself?"

"No. You mean after shifting?"

"That's one time."

I sighed and chuckled a little. "That certainly could have come in handy over the years. Walking naked into a village has never really been considered polite."

"Depends on the village," Frances answered with a smirk. "But I get your point. I've been able to make simple clothes from natural fibers pulled from the earth."

"Even here, in the desert?"

"Even here. They will travel through the earth. And when you're done with them, you put them back. A constant circle."

"Okay. I'm ready."

"Close your eyes, envision what you want the clothing to look like. I'll go first. You can use my same spell or come up with one of your own." Frances looked to me for confirmation, and I nodded. Focusing back on his task, he closed his eyes and held his hand out. "Mother Earth, nurturer of man. Send your great fingers searching, gathering, collecting. Bring me cotton, bring me wool from lamb. Bind and form until they cling. Dress me to cover who I am. Clothe me until once again I take wing."

Watching carefully, I could see hundreds, thousands, millions of tiny fibers collecting, gathering together. They came from the earth itself, binding together until Frances held an outfit in his hand.

He took hold of it and shook it out while I stared in amazement. "Pants and a shirt. Not bad."

"Your turn."

"All right." Closing my eyes, I concentrated. Felt the earth through the soles of my feet. Holding my hands out as Frances had, I said, "Mother Earth, strong and true. I seek cotton, I seek wool, I seek silk. Search and gather, bind and form; this I ask of you. Clothe me from prying eyes; show me what you've built."

Soft weight landed in my hands, and I snuck a peak at what I'd wrought. A simple cotton dress, dark blue like the night sky above. Frances looked at it, impressed. "Nice job. It almost seemed like you've done this before. You even got a color."

"Not on purpose. I only thought of a dress."

"She probably likes you more than she likes me."

I stared at him, wondering where that had come from. "You've atoned for your sins. Do you still have trouble with the elements?"

"It's not as easy as it was. Like a strained relationship—what I imagine it would be like if a man cheated on his wife. She still loves me; I can feel that, but the trust is gone." He'd been staring at the ground, but now he looked at me, fierce in his quest. "I will continue to prove my worth until she trusts me again."

Swallowing hard, I wondered what I could say. I no longer looked at Frances, the saved shadowman; I simply saw Frances, the man. One who struggled with the sins of his past. "I know you will. You've done so well so far."

"Thanks," he mumbled, then brightened. "So, what else should we try?"

Chapter 3

Frances and I arrived home before the sun made its appearance. He closed himself off in his room while I spent the morning reading. Prior to lunch, there was a knock on the door, and I checked through the peephole before answering. For a brief moment, I considered pretending I wasn't home, but I didn't think that would stop Samson.

When I opened the door, he grinned, and it gave him an air of mischief. "Good morning,"

"Good morning," I returned hesitantly, keeping the door partially closed. "What are you doing here?"

"I came to give you these," he said, bringing one hand out from behind his back with a flourish. In his fist, he held a bouquet of wildflowers. "And to keep asking you to lunch until you say yes."

"Persistent, aren't you?" I murmured, fighting with myself over how to handle this. The baser part of myself, the part that knew this man was my mate, attempted to claw its way out and claim him.

The rest of me, the part that had been wandering the earth for years with no family or friends, wanted to run in the other direction.

"Oh, give the guy a break," said a voice from inside the house. The door pulled all the way open, leaving me stumbling for balance. Frances grinned out at Samson. "Hey, man."

"Hey, Frances. My family's doing a little cookout later today if you'd like to stop by."

"Sounds fun. Lani will go with you now, and I'll meet up with you later."

They both turned to look at me, and I let out a frustrated groan. "Fine. I'll be right back."

Frances invited Samson inside, and as they settled into our new chairs, I stomped off to my room. I'd been wearing comfortable clothes, as I hadn't planned on leaving the house anytime soon, and I wanted to change into something more appropriate.

Pulling open the small closet, I stared at my collection of clothes and had a sudden shortness of breath. I had nothing to wear!

Pacing away, I placed both palms against my temples and applied pressure. I was being ridiculous. This was just a lunch outing; anything I wore would be fine. For a moment, I considered calling Jade to get her advice, but I wasn't ready to tell her about Samson. Telling her would be admitting it to myself, and I *really* wasn't ready for that.

Determined now, I marched back to the closet and selected the first thing I saw. As I began pulling the shorts and shirt off the hanger,

I hesitated and switched it out for a sundress. The day had already turned hot, and a dress would be more appropriate.

Not because I wanted to impress Samson.

Stepping into the bathroom, I examined myself in the mirror. I didn't typically wear much makeup and left it that way. My hair hung long and thick, so I quickly braided it over my shoulder. The sky-blue dress not only fit like a glove but set off my golden skin tone nicely.

Though I was relatively tall at five foot nine, I felt comfortable selecting a pair of small heels, knowing I still wouldn't match Samson's height.

Sucking in a breath, I stepped out of the room and walked the few short steps down the hall to the living area. Samson looked up, pausing mid-sentence, his eyes bugging out. Somewhere deep inside, in a purely feminine part of me, I thoroughly enjoyed his reaction.

He stood quickly, suddenly fumbling for words. "Wow. You look good. I mean, you look amazing. Beautiful. You're beautiful."

"Thank you," I said, amused. He still held the bunch of flowers, so I pointed in question. "Want me to take those?"

"Sure," he said, shoving the bundle toward me.

Taking them into the kitchen, I dug a glass out of the cupboard. We didn't have any vases, so it would have to do. Leaving them on the counter, I spoke to Frances. "Will you be able to get the table on your own?"

"Sure, no problem."

“Okay, I guess I’m ready,” I said to Samson.

“You kids have fun,” Frances said with a wink. I glared in response.

“Do you mind if we walk?” Samson asked once we stepped outside. “I enjoy being outdoors, and I have a feeling you do, too.”

“I don’t mind. Where are we headed?”

“There are only a couple of restaurants in town and only one really worth eating at.”

We walked together in companionable silence. Every once in a while, Samson’s hand brushed against mine, shooting tingles of awareness through all my nerve endings. It was impossible to tell if he felt it, too. He hummed under his breath, which felt oddly soothing.

“Have you always lived here?”

“I have, my family has for as far back as we can go.”

“Does it ever get boring?”

“Not when beautiful, mysterious women come to town.” I shot him a look and found him grinning playfully at me. He made it difficult to even pretend to be upset. “I’ve traveled some, would like to do more. Until now, I had a feeling that I was exactly where I was supposed to be.”

“Why do you think that is?”

He looked at me again, waited for me to meet his eye. “Because I was waiting for you.”

"Samson—"

"Sorry, sorry. Except I'm not sorry. I might be bungling this up a little; you took me by surprise. But tell me you don't feel it, too."

"It doesn't matter what I feel. What matters is what's best for you."

"It does matter." Samson stopped abruptly and scooped up my hands with his. I stared at him, helpless to do anything else. "You matter. To me, even if you think no one else cares. I do. I always have."

"What do you mean?"

"I'll explain later. Are you hungry?"

The abrupt topic change left me whirling. What had I agreed to? "Yes."

"Great, me too. You like spicy food?" Releasing one hand, Samson kept hold of the other as we continued toward the main road. His hand engulfed mine, his temperature nearly as warm as my own. Every once in a while, his thumb would brush a caress over my sensitized skin.

"I can handle heat."

"Good," he said with another of his signature grins. He led the way to a small restaurant and pulled out a seat at one of the spattering of tables. "Have a seat, m'lady."

Shaking my head at his antics, I sat, smoothing my dress under my legs. The owner came over, shook Samson's hand, and asked after his family. The chef shouted a greeting from the kitchen. Part of me felt a strange longing for the familiarity.

"Jorge, this is Lani. She says she can handle heat."

"That so? Well, I'll fix you right up. Anything you don't like?"

"Not really," I said.

"Two chef specials it is. What can I get you to drink?"

"Water for me."

"Make that two. Thanks, buddy." Samson slid into his seat and relaxed back. "How are you settling in?"

"Just fine. Didn't have much to unpack."

"Where are you coming from?"

"Wisconsin."

"Long way. Do you miss it?"

"Some things. People, more."

"How long were you there? I get the feeling you move around a bit," he added at my arched look.

"Just under a year. And you're right, I do."

Jorge brought over drinks, chips, and salsa. "This is a hot batch."

"Thanks," I said, dipping a chip to try it out. The heat slid down my throat and settled in my belly. "It's good."

Jorge winked and went back to the kitchen. Samson tried some, nodded. "That's the stuff. What made you decide to come here?"

Back to the questioning. I decided to give him as much of the truth as I could without opening a whole new can of worms. "I'm looking for some of my family."

"And you think they might be around here?"

"I was hoping I'd find someone who might be able to point me in the right direction."

Samson sat back and studied me carefully. "You're evading."

"A little. I'm afraid if I fully answer your questions, you're only going to have a thousand more."

"Okay, we'll backtrack a little. What's your favorite color?"

Laughing, I shook my head. "You really are easy going, aren't you?"

"We're going to have a lot to talk about. Later. I get that you're not ready yet. Maybe I'm not either. For now, I won't push you."

Where had this man come from? Anyone else would be freaking out about our first encounter and asking endless questions. Why wasn't he? What was he hiding? Taking a breath, I took a chance. "Orange. But dark, closer to burnt orange or bronze."

"Mine's blue." His eyes dropped, lifted back to mine. "Like your dress. The color of the desert sky at high noon."

We shared a smile as Jorge brought out two plates of food.

Conversing with Samson was surprisingly easy. Whenever we broached a subject that I wasn't comfortable with, he'd instantly back off and throw out another off-the-wall question. He joked, and I laughed. A lot.

After we devoured our lunch, Samson took me on a town tour. He showed me the school he'd attended and the community center. He waved at every person that passed—whether on foot or by car—and shouted personal greetings to any who could hear. In a way, Mescalero reminded me of Sun Valley; small, friendly.

We walked back to pick up Frances, then headed to Samson's parents' for the barbecue. Already, a large group had gathered in the backyard, everyone seemingly oblivious to the hot temps. We stopped at the grill, where a man that could easily be Samson in another thirty years flipped burgers.

"Lani, Frances, these are my parents—Neveah and Santiago. Over there is my sister, Raven."

"Frances!" Nova shouted from across the yard. Dragging an identical girl along with, Nova bounded over and hugged Frances. "This is my sister, Tala."

"My cousins," Samson supplied. "Their older brothers, Atienn and Chayton, are over there, and their parents, Emilia and Domingo, are over there."

"What'd I tell you? He's so pretty." Nova grinned conspiratorially at her sister. "Who do you think we could set him up with?"

Simultaneously they said, "Valentina!" before bursting into a fit of giggles. Before Frances could reply, they were off, dragging him in their wake. I might have enjoyed his predicament a little more than necessary.

"Poor Valentina," Samson said with a chuckle. "She's my best friend's younger sister. We consider them family, and I'm sure there are some blood ties if we look far enough back. Speaking of—there's Josiah, and his wife, Tayen."

Feeling a little overwhelmed by all the introductions, I greeted the tall man with buzzed cut hair who had his arm wrapped around a petite woman, her long hair piled artfully atop her head.

"Nice to meet you," Josiah said, shaking my hand. He shared an approving look with Samson, and my eyes narrowed in suspicion. That, and the fact that everyone I'd met so far seemed to be Gifted. I'd never come across such a large group before. "I see Samson annoyed you into coming today."

"He's relentless," I agreed.

While they chuckled, Viktor approached with a woman I took to be his wife, along with four little girls. Viktor introduced me to Niko, who, in turn, told me the girls' names. "My niece, Kai. Our daughters, Kateri, Koko, and Kaiah."

Kai looked to be the oldest, around twelve, while the younger three looked no more than a few years apart. "Nice to meet you. How old are you?"

"I'm twelve," Kai confirmed.

Kateri answered for herself and her sisters. "I'm ten, Koko's nine, and Kaiah's eight."

They all grinned widely, and I couldn't help but return the gesture. I could almost feel the power emanating from all four; even at so young an age, I knew they all had powerful abilities.

Since we'd just met, and Samson and I hadn't even had that particular conversation yet, I decided to hold my tongue. Even if I couldn't be a true mate to Samson, I couldn't turn away from the fact that his family all carried the Gifted gene. They might need help to understand what they possessed.

"Are you thirsty?" Kai asked. "We can show you where the drinks are."

"That would be lovely," I said. Then, before I could even glance at Samson, they grabbed my arms and began dragging me across the yard. Must be a family trait.

"Are you Samson's girlfriend?" Koko asked, earning a nudge from her older sister. Kateri looked just as interested in the answer, though.

"We're friends," I said, much to their disappointment. "Has he had many girlfriends?"

"None," Koko answered with a giggle. "He was waiting for you."

"Koko," Kateri hissed. "Shut up!"

"Why? It's true."

"You're going to scare her off," Kai said, the voice of reason.

Smiling gently, I lowered my voice as well. "I'm not that easy to scare."

"True," said a new voice from behind me. Turning, I recognized the woman Samson had identified earlier as his sister. "Though I have a feeling you'd feel more comfortable fighting a big, burly man than making small talk with a group of strangers."

"Also true," I said. "You're Raven."

"That I am. Nice to meet you. Why don't you grab a drink, and we can take a little walk?"

Though the girls looked disappointed, I promised to come find them later. Following Raven across the backyard and down a slight hill, we paused at a well-used dirt path that wound around the base of the mountains. "Beautiful spot."

"I walk here every day. Early in the morning or as the sun sets. Too hot otherwise." Raven took a sip of her drink and studied me over the rim of her glass. "I hope you don't plan on hurting my brother."

"Does one ever plan such a thing?"

"I suppose not. The thing is, he's waited a long time for you. We're all very close—as you can see. You'd have all of us to deal with if you did."

"The last thing I would ever want is for Samson to be hurt in any way." She couldn't ignore the ring of truth in my words. It was there, plain as day. "But the best thing for him might be me staying away."

"You don't give him much credit if you truly believe that. Samson is stronger than you know. Than most know. Where you see a laid-back, easygoing guy, the truth is he'd go to bat for me, for you, for anyone he cares about." Raven met my gaze head-on, a strange sort of intensity burning in her eyes. "Don't underestimate him, Lani. Or any of us."

My heart began to pound in my chest. Agreeing to lunch, to this cookout—it had been a mistake. Samson deserved so much better than me.

"Lani?"

Samson appeared at the top of the hill, looking anxiously at Raven and me. I sucked in a breath, refusing to look at him. To Raven, I muttered, "I'm sorry. I shouldn't have come."

Turning away from them both, I began to run. Blurring my image when I got far enough, I used my preternatural speed to go far, far away. Even Samson's echoing shouts couldn't sway me.

I had to go. I never should have come.

Chapter 4

The first time Samson had a dream that wasn't a dream, he'd been barely more than a babe. His dream girl, as he'd come to think of her, had haunted his sleeping and waking hours for his entire life.

When his mom saw him drawing pictures of the same woman over and over, he finally told her why. And instead of blaming an overactive imagination or television, she believed him. When Samson realized he wouldn't be ridiculed or doubted, he told his dad and sister, Raven. Eventually, his entire family knew the story of Samson's dream girl.

He put up with the ridicule from boys his age when all they could talk about was girls, and he wanted nothing to do with it. He still went out with his friends—mostly Josiah—and even took a date to a few high school dances, but he made it clear before and during that it was and would only ever be as friends. Most of the girls didn't believe him at first, but eventually, they came to think of Samson in the same capacity as having a gay best friend.

Samson didn't mind the comparison and was able to ignore the majority of the teasing that came out of it. He didn't care because he had his family, his best friend, and the idea that one day, his dream girl would come into his life.

When she did, Samson had been completely knocked off his feet—figuratively and literally. She'd saved him, as she'd saved so many others. Selflessly. Heedless of her own health and safety, asking for nothing in return.

He'd seen her do the same throughout the years, every time he connected to her memories. She seemed to be having an identity crisis, but Samson had no doubt about who Lani was.

And he'd completely bungled it. He'd pushed too hard, too fast, and Lani had run. He would blame himself later, but now, he had a much more convenient target. When Lani became nothing more than a dot on the horizon, Samson glared at his sister. "What did you say to her?"

"I told her the truth," Raven said, throwing her hands up. "Obviously, she couldn't handle it."

"I can't believe you! Do you have any idea what it took for her to come here today? To face her fears?"

"Oh, please. We're not scary."

"Not to you, but to her? She can face down the evil in the world without flinching, but when it comes to a family like ours, it's the most terrifying thing she can imagine. She has spent her life avoiding making connections, avoiding emotional ties, and the second she dips her toes, you attack her.”

“No, Samson, I—”

He was too angry to hear her out. “I need to go. I need to find her.”

Frances delicately cleared his throat and reached out to put a hand on Samson’s shoulder. “Let me. I’ll find her, talk her off the ledge. Give her a little bit of time, and she’ll come back to you.”

“You promise?”

Samson’s eyes were wild, scared. Frances felt a part of him, long thought dead, take pity on the man. “I promise.”

“Samson—” Raven tried again, but Samson brushed her off.

“I don’t want to talk to you right now.” And before either of them could say anything more, Samson walked away.

He didn’t have a destination in mind, but he didn’t feel like spending the afternoon pretending to be in a good mood. Going home didn’t hold much appeal, either. Against Frances’ advice, Samson had every intention of going after Lani. They had a strong connection that made him believe he could find her.

All but decided, Samson headed toward the front of the house so he could loop around back toward the desert while avoiding his family. When he thought he was in the clear, he heard his mom’s voice. “Where are you going?”

"I'm not in a party mood right now," he said, not bothering to face her.

"Samson." She waited, and with a sigh, Samson turned. Neveah studied her son for a few moments before nodding to herself. "Before you leave, would you mind helping me carry out the extra table and chairs?"

Samson knew there was no getting around his duty to his mom. He followed her inside and to his old bedroom, which now served as a guestroom and storage. Neveah pulled open the closet doors and started carting boxes out of the way. When she grunted under the weight of one, Samson quickly grabbed it. "What is all this?"

"Take a look," Neveah said, gesturing for him to set the box down on the bed.

When he popped open the lid, Samson pulled out a binder and looked inside. His mom had taken mementos from his childhood—report cards, essays, artwork—and organized them in plastic sleeves. He flipped through a few sleeves until all of the drawings of Lani he'd made over the years stared back at him. "You kept all this?"

"Of course. These are yours, and I have ones for Raven as well." She brushed a light fingertip over one of the drawings and watched him carefully. "You were such a special boy, and you have grown into a wonderful man. Other mothers thought I should worry about your lack of interest in relationships, but I never did. Did I ever tell you about when I met your father?"

"He was a year older in school, and you were both in sports, right?"

"That is true, yes. Your dad, he was the star of the soccer team. Brought the team to state his junior and senior year. But in the finals his senior year, the deciding game, he got injured."

Samson cocked his head. "I've never heard that."

"Because no one else knew," she said with a smile. "He rolled his ankle and went down. The coaches put on an ice pack and were waiting for the paramedics when I marched right onto the field and knelt at his side. It was the first time he'd ever seen me—or ever noticed me, at least. When our eyes met that night, we both knew he was mine, and I was his. There would be no other for us.

"I put my palms on his ankle and said, 'Do you trust me?' He nodded, just like that. It was the first time I used my healing power on someone other than close family. The coaches were yelling at me to leave, and the paramedics were running toward us, and we both ignored them all. When I took my hands off, he stood, good as new, took my hand, and kissed it."

"What did the coaches and paramedics do?"

"Nothing. They figured his injury hadn't been as bad as they thought, so I got off the field, and they played the rest of the game. The second the game was done, your dad ran into the bleachers where I was sitting and asked me my name and if I would go to the movies with him that weekend. I said yes."

She smiled softly, remembering the feeling of first love. Santiago was her first and only love, and she saw the same connection between her son and the mysterious woman who had shown up in their lives seemingly out of the blue. Samson took his mom's hand between his. "That's a really nice story. Thank you for sharing it with me."

"This is Lani, isn't it?"

Samson glanced down at the drawings once more. "It is. I can't explain it, but it is."

"Our family, we have magic in the blood. She has it, too. Different than ours. Power oozes from her, but sadness, too. There is much she is dealing with. Things that may take time."

"I know. I know I pushed too far, too fast. I need to back off."

Neveah shook her head. "I don't think that's the right answer, either."

"Then what do I do?"

"You be who you are. Caring, honest. Unfailingly supportive. You bring joy to every life you touch. Don't be pushy, but don't back down, either. She needs someone dependable, someone stable. A constant. She has not had that in her life, and it will take some time for her to trust that you will not disappear."

"Just be myself," Samson said with a wry smile. "I guess that could work."

"Mothers know best. Now, help me with that table, make up with your sister, and go find your girl."

Samson kissed his mom on the cheek and set out to follow her orders. After setting up the table, he sought out Raven, who sat by herself with a sulky expression. She wouldn't look at him when he settled beside her, and he didn't expect her to speak first. "I'm sorry I yelled."

"I might have deserved a bit of it."

"Will you make things right with Lani?"

Raven nodded. "It's the least I can do."

"She's important to me, Raven."

Now, she did look at him. "How can you know? You met her two days ago."

"When it's right, you know." He held up his hands to ward off any argument. "For *our* family, when it's right, we know."

"That's not very helpful."

Samson studied his sister much as his mom had done to him. Though she was only two years younger, Samson had always thought of her as his baby sister. While he would always be protective of her, he realized she was a grown ass woman who, like him, had never had any kind of relationship. "You've never been attracted to anyone, have you?"

Startled, Raven's wide eyes shot to Samson before fixating on the table. "No, I haven't."

"There's nothing wrong with that, you know. I never was either."

"Yeah, but you knew you'd meet her one day. You had the dreams. I have nothing."

"That's not true. Raven—"

Samson reached out, but Raven stood abruptly and waved a hand in his general direction. "I need some time alone. I'll find Lani tomorrow, okay?"

"Yeah, sure." He watched her retreat and continued to sit alone, his mind racing with thoughts of Raven and Lani. Despite the reassurances from his mom, Samson still wondered if giving Lani space would be the better move.

Glancing across the yard to where his parents stole a kiss when they thought no one was looking, he knew that he wanted that with every breath in his body. Lani held the answers to every question he'd ever had about his own life. She may even hold the answers his sister needed.

He knew he could find Lani right now, and the majority of him wanted to do just that, but the logical part of his brain finally won out and told him to follow Frances' advice first. He would let her cousin talk to her, and when she returned, Samson would be there.

He didn't care how long he would have to wait.

Chapter 5

*L*ani. Closing my eyes, I ignored the soft, questioning tone. My special gift could be such an inconvenience when I needed to be alone. *Lani, just tell me you're okay.*

Still, I didn't respond. It had been hours since I'd left the barbecue. I'd run in human form, then as a leopard. Farther and farther away. I needed to think, to breathe. Eventually, I'd looped back around. While in the past I might have kept going, avoiding it all, I had responsibility now. Frances, for one. I'd promised Jade and Talon that I would look over him. A job I'd committed to.

And then there was Samson.

Sighing, I ran my hands through my hair and then used them to prop my chin up. Finding my mate complicated matters. As I gazed out over the gently rolling dunes, washed in the light of the nearly full moon, I wondered at the timing of it. Why here, why now? All these years, a century or more, I'd lived alone. Lost and alone.

Now, I felt as if I was on the cusp of finding my family. My brother, at least. Perhaps, finding him, I would get my memories back. Samson's appearance just threw me for a loop.

Soft steps alerted me to another's presence. Not feet, but paws. Padding nearly silently up the steep cliff overlooking the town, I sighed and looked over as Frances transformed into his human form and settled beside me.

"Nice spot."

"How'd you find me?"

He lifted his palm, showing me one of my favorite necklaces. "Locater spell."

Snatching the jewelry away, I let out a breath. "You'll have to teach me that one."

"You've got the clothes one down," he said, gesturing toward my simple outfit. "I was worried about you. So is Samson, and Raven feels terrible. Why'd you run off?"

"I don't belong here."

"I'd say you do."

"No, Frances, you don't get it. I have no idea who I am. I've only seen evil in the world; I've been fighting it for more than a lifetime. And now, Samson just expects me to be with him?"

"Did he say that?"

"He didn't have to."

"I think you should ask him."

"Ask him what?"

"What he wants. What he expects from you. I think you'd be surprised by the answer."

"Go away, Frances."

"Nah, I'm good right here." He leaned back on his elbows and gazed up at the moon. "Beautiful night."

"If you won't leave, I will."

"Go ahead. It's a free country. But before you go, you should know something."

"What?"

"I'm here for you. That's what friends do. If you tell me you hate Samson—which I won't believe, seeing as he's your mate—then we can leave tomorrow. If you need time, I'll help you tell him that. But the one thing I won't do? I won't leave you alone."

I stared at him, wondering at the utter sincerity in his voice. At that moment, he was no longer the annoying former shadowman I'd been coerced into babysitting. He was a man sitting next to his friend in the moonlight. Quietly, I said, "Thank you."

We continued to sit, silence settling over us. It was the comfortable kind, the kind that said more than words. The turmoil that had been rumbling inside me settled, smoothed. I no longer felt the need to run. "Frances? What happened to your family?" He stayed quiet so long I didn't think he'd answer. "It's all right if you don't want to talk about it."

"No, it's fine. It's just...difficult." I waited as he gathered his courage. From Jade, I knew something terrible had happened to Frances, his family, when he'd been a young boy. His path to darkness began the day he lost his parents. "I was born to a powerful family in Malta in the sixteen-hundreds. My twin sister—Alessia—and I were trained practically from birth to take over for our parents."

"Take over? How?"

He sucked in a breath, let it out again. "They were the rulers of Malta. Fair, kind, just rulers. When I was six, there was a revolt. Many died...my parents included. Alessia and I escaped through a network of tunnels. We survived on our own for three years."

"You were so young."

"Young, but powerful. We were not human children, Lani. We were Elementals with an extensive background in survival and leadership. We didn't have much of a childhood, but it ended up saving our lives. I didn't realize it at the time, or even in the years since, but ever since Jade freed me, I've come to realize that those who staged the uprising were shadowmen posing as advisors and loyal subjects."

The story wasn't over. I knew he'd lost his sister, too. It's what pushed him over the edge into darkness.

"I always felt responsible for Alessia, even though we were the same age. She had a goodness about her I lacked, even at that age.

Even before the revolt. I was always the serious one. I think I was born with a shadow of darkness inside me. Perhaps all male Elementals are.

"We kept moving across Europe. Eventually, a band of gypsies took us in. They moved around enough that the shadowmen chasing us were thwarted. I used my magic to keep all of us safe as best I could. Then one night...." He took a moment to collect himself. I had a feeling he hadn't told anyone this story in a long time. Perhaps ever. "Three years had gone by, and we hadn't had any trouble. I knew that was because we constantly moved and because I used my magic. But Alessia—she felt closed in. She thought we were safe, that whoever had chased us was long gone."

He paused then, his breath hitching in his throat. I reached over and placed my hand over his. "You don't have to tell me."

"I want to. Someone should know. Alessia formed a close bond with one of the boys in the group. He was a few years older, and she looked at him with stars in her eyes. He convinced her to go swimming one night as the adults slept. I told her she couldn't, that she had to stay in the safety of the camp. I should have known she wouldn't listen. When she breached the safety net of my magic, I woke and tried to find her. By the time I reached the swimming spot, I found the boy dead and Alessia gone."

"Frances," I said, further words escaping me. "I'm so sorry."

"What's done is done. I remember screaming over and over. I couldn't reach her through our twin link. I blamed the boy, even though he was dead. I hated him. The adults came, and I ran. I think they always attributed his death to me. I didn't care.

"For a long time, I wandered on my own. That time is a blur now. I was so filled with anger, resentment. Crushing loneliness and despair."

None of it excused his acceptance of the dark, but now I understood how it happened. That poor boy, all alone. Blaming himself for the death of his parents, his sister. "It wasn't your fault, Frances. You did more than any other boy could have done."

"I know that, logically. But in here?" He tapped his chest, looked out across the barren earth. "I still blame myself."

We fell back into silence. Neither of us had any more to say. Something had shifted between us, though. A deeper understanding and mutual respect. As the evening turned into night, I stood and wiped the dirt from my pants. "I'd like to go home now."

Frances nodded and stood. "Should we run or fly?"

Smiling, I answered, "Let's walk."

"Boring, but dealer's choice. Let's go."

We scaled the rocky terrain together. Frances offered me his hand over particularly difficult spots. Instead of pointing out that I could float over them—or plow right through—I simply accepted his help and moved on.

Walking at a normal human pace, it took us over an hour to return home. A figure lounged on the steps, his back against the front door. I shouldn't have been surprised—Samson had proven to be more than determined—but I did feel my heart give a little lurch.

Exchanging a look with Frances, he gave me a nod and a small smile before slipping away. I walked over to Samson and crouched before him. He slept, his breath light and even. Laying a hand against his arm, I nudged gently. "Samson."

He woke with a start, then settled on seeing me. He breathed a sigh of relief. "Lani. Are you okay?"

"I'm fine, but you won't be if you stay in this position any longer." Helping him up, I unlocked the door and stepped inside. I glanced at the living room furniture, then down the hall. Neither seemed like a great spot to sit and talk. "Why don't we go out back? Do you want something to drink?"

"Do you have anything stronger than water?"

"I think Frances stocked up on some beer," I said, going to the fridge and grabbing two. I didn't normally drink—alcohol burned off rather quickly with my higher temperature—but it seemed like a good prop for the conversation we were about to have. "After you."

Following Samson outside, I handed him a bottle and settled beside him on a worn loveseat-style piece of furniture. We took a few sips in silence, the night quiet and cool in the absence of sun.

"I'm sorry for leaving so quickly. Your family must think I'm very rude."

"I should be the one apologizing. They were too much, too soon. Raven feels terrible. She's just overprotective and has a hard time believing you're...."

When he trailed off, I looked over at him and frowned. "I'm what?"

"You're going to think I'm crazy," Samson said, pulling a hand through his thick hair.

"I doubt that. Just tell me."

Letting out a breath, he turned to face me head-on. "I dreamt of you."

"Last night?"

"No," he said, shaking his head emphatically. "Since I was a child."

Surprise ran through me, momentarily leaving me speechless. His eyes searched mine nervously, waiting for me to respond. Unsure how to proceed, I asked, "Um...what kind of dreams?"

"You don't think I'm crazy?"

"Not yet."

That coaxed out half a smile. "The dreams were all different. I was never in them; it was more like—it was more like I *was* you, living out your life."

My surprise turned to shock as I quickly ran the possibilities through my mind. Jade had once told me that she dreamt of Talon—

or, more accurately, she connected to his memories while she slept. She described it as living out his life.

"You don't believe me." Samson slumped against the seat, looking as if he wanted to take it back.

"Well, it does sound a little far-fetched, but—"

Before I could continue, Samson interrupted me. "In one of them, you were walking through a forest, unlike anything I've seen. You came across a small girl at a stream who had been crying. You spoke to her, asked what was wrong. She told you her father was dead, her mother sick with the same disease. You told her it would be all right and to bring you to her village."

My heart lodged in my throat as I listened to a tale no one could know. It had happened over a century ago, and I hadn't spoken of it since.

"She brought you to her village where a disease had wiped out most of the population. There were piles of the dead, waiting to be buried, but not enough healthy people to see it done. You went into the small shack that was the girl's home and found her mother near death. You gave her your blood. After a few minutes, her eyes opened, and she said..."

"You are an angel. Bless you," I whispered.

Samson nodded. "You went through the village and continued to heal all who were sick, then helped to bury the bodies and eradicate the disease. They called you *ángel de la vida*."

"The angel of life," I translated. When our eyes met again, something new passed between us. It would be pointless now to hide anything from him, though the crazy table may take a turn. "Samson, there's something I have to tell you."

"All right," he said, still waiting for me to turn against him.

"I'm...I'm not like other people."

His mouth tipped up at the edge. "Obviously."

"It's more than what happened on the job site yesterday."

"I know. You rescued me. An impossible rescue, and then you simply disappeared. And if those dreams were true—I mean, you gave those people your blood. Not by transfusion but by mouth. Also, the way they were dressed...that didn't happen in modern times, did it?"

"Oh," I said, realizing Samson knew much more than I gave him credit for. "How are you not completely freaked out by this?"

"Supernatural phenomenon isn't exactly new in my life," he answered wryly.

"What do you mean?"

He hesitated, then grinned. "Oh, no. We're not on me yet. This is about you."

We'd get back to that, then. I sucked in a breath, let it out, and began my story—my real story. "I am more than human; a creature of nature and magic. I don't know where I was born or who my family is. One day, I woke up in a forest in South America with no memory of who I'd been."

"Lani," Samson said, gripping my hand in support. "You must have been terrified."

I let his warmth seep into me, comforting and strong. "Confused, yes. Worried, yes. Terrified? I don't think I ever was. Lost, alone, afraid sometimes, but not as extreme as I should have been. I was too concerned with surviving.

"The first time I came across someone like me—more than human—I was so excited I forgot to be on guard. He turned out to be an evil creature, one that had to be eradicated from the earth. I learned my most important lesson that day: that I could trust no one but myself."

After a quiet moment, I continued to talk. Told him of my nomadic years. Moving every few months to stay off the radar. And finally, finally, meeting Jade. Talon. Realizing I wasn't alone, didn't have to be alone anymore. "Talon suggested I come here. He lived off the land as a boy with his mother and father. He thought I could find others like us."

"And what are you?" Samson asked. He'd stayed quiet during my story, his free hand tracing patterns over mine.

"A lost and confused woman. I know you feel the connection between us. I do, too. But Samson, I can't give you more than what I am. I can't—"

His finger pressed against my lips. "Hush. You are amazing and beautiful, and I feel like the luckiest man in the world to even know you. You need time; I can give you time. You want me to help you find your family? I'll do that, too. But don't ever think you aren't good enough."

I stared up at him, feeling every one of my tense muscles relax with his words, his gentle caresses. He truly wasn't asking for anything more than I could give him. We were close, so close. His lips just inches away.

He leaned down, and I braced for him to make contact with mine. He didn't. His lips brushed against my forehead, and his arm wrapped around my back so that my head could rest against his shoulder. He said nothing more; neither did I. For tonight, this was enough.

Chapter 6

I shouldn't have slept. There was no reason to. I hadn't battled that day, and it was night—my time. Yet I found myself blinking the world back into focus as the sun broke past the horizon and shot across the sky.

Samson and I hadn't moved, not really. He'd slouched down, one arm still around my back, the other still gripping my hand. Nothing about our position should have been comfortable, yet I never wanted to move.

"Good morning," he murmured, his eyes still closed.

"Good morning. Are you all right? This can't be comfortable enough to sleep on."

"Just fine." He shifted, brought me fully against his chest. "Even better."

Laughing, I wrapped an arm around his waist and squeezed. "We should really get up."

"Why?"

"How about breakfast?"

One eye popped open, looked down at me. "Breakfast?"

"I'm not a gourmet chef, but I can scramble an egg."

"Throw in some bacon and coffee, and I'm sold."

"Lucky for you, I have both." I stood and pulled him up with me. When I went inside, Frances was nowhere to be seen.

"Early riser, or still sleeping?" Samson asked, gesturing toward his door with a thumb.

"He doesn't sleep much." I got out the pans I'd need and ingredients from the fridge. I was glad I'd thought to stock it the night we'd moved in. "Do you take cream, sugar?"

"Both," Samson said. "You?"

"Neither."

He loaded the coffee and poured in filtered water. "Interesting. Favorite kind of eggs?"

"Scrambled, with lots of vegetables." I chopped some as I spoke, the bacon already sizzling in the pan. "You?"

"Over easy, but a veggie scramble works just as well. My choice is more laziness in the kitchen than preference."

"Not a big cook?"

"Not usually, unless the mood strikes. Just as easy to finagle a meal out of my mom."

I laughed, then said, "It's nice that you're all so close."

"It is. I know they can be overwhelming at first, but I promise they're good people."

"They remind me of my friend Jade's family. Big, intrusive. They were always setting her up with random men before she met Talon."

"I can't wait to meet them." Glancing over at him, I was temporarily at a loss for words. This seemed so easy, so natural. Light conversation while cooking breakfast.

So normal.

"You will. They're headed this way, hopefully soon." Taking out the bacon, I threw the vegetables in and gave them a toss in the leftover grease. As I pulled out a bowl and began cracking eggs, Samson snuck a piece of bacon, and I slapped his hand away with a laugh. "Should have known."

"It's better the truth came out now. I'm a bad boy."

Rolling my eyes, I whipped the eggs and poured in some of the cream Samson used in his coffee to make them fluffy. "I have no doubt."

"Did I miss breakfast?" Frances called out from the living room. He entered the kitchen wearing workout clothes, though I doubted that's what he'd been doing.

"You're just in time," I said, adding a few more eggs to the bowl. "And good morning."

Samson grabbed three plates and set the newly acquired table. "Did you go for a run?"

"Yup. Didn't get this body by lounging around."

Samson shook his head and playfully punched him in the arm. "We'll get some real muscles on you on the job."

At the knock on the door, Frances and I exchanged a look. Expanding my senses, I made sure there was no threat. Frances did the same and then answered the door. "Raven. Good morning."

"Hi," she said. "Is Lani here?"

"Hey, sis," Samson said. "What are you doing here?"

"I came to see Lani." When I came around the corner, Raven breathed out a sigh of relief. "You are here. I'm so, so sorry. Here, this is for you."

Taking the container that she shoved into my hands, I lifted the lid and was assaulted by the scent of barbecue sauce and charcoal smoke. "Leftovers?"

"You never got to eat yesterday. And seriously, so, so sorry. Again."

"You have nothing to be sorry for, but thank you for coming over. Would you like to join us for breakfast?"

"I'd love to," Raven said with a relieved smile but then glanced at Samson and hesitated. "Are we good?"

He wrapped one arm around her shoulders. "We're good."

I went back to the stove, threw in more vegetables, and then the eggs. Samson poured coffee all around. Once the eggs finished cooking, I divided it into four and sat with them at the table. Samson and Raven were obviously close, something Frances and I both envied. Or missed.

Frances had a sister, as I had a brother. I didn't remember mine, besides the one memory Jade had been able to unlock, but with that one memory came a wealth of emotions I had no basis and no life experiences for. Watching the easy exchanges, the constant, friendly ribbing, and the love shining between them made me ache just a little.

When we were done, the men handled the dishes, much to Frances' detriment. I walked Raven out, wanting to speak with her alone. "I'm sorry for leaving the way I did last night."

"No, that's on me. I shouldn't have threatened you."

"You love your brother, and you want what's best for him. I'm not sure that's me, but it seems the universe has other ideas." I stayed quiet a moment, looking at my feet. "He told me about his dreams."

Raven sucked in a breath. I looked her in the eye, letting her see how seriously I took the matter. "And you believed him?"

"I did. I can't explain it, but he knew things about me I've never told anyone. There are some things I have to speak with him about first, but I want you to know I understand your concern. The thing is, I will do everything in my power to protect him. Even if I have to protect him from me."

She nodded and pulled me in for a hug. "Thanks, Lani. For forgiving me and for telling me this. I'll always have Samson's back, but I'll have yours, too."

Stepping back, I smiled and bid her goodbye. Raven had a special gift; it burned brightly in her dark eyes. While I wondered what it was, I also knew she didn't trust me nearly enough to tell me. I needed to work on my relationship with Samson first. Dealing with his Gifted family would come later.

When I walked back in, the dishes were almost done. Placing a hand on Frances' back, I said, "I'll take it from here."

He nodded and happily disappeared into his room. Samson handed me a freshly rinsed dish and asked, "Everything okay with you and Raven?"

"It is now. I'm glad she came over."

"Me, too. It's important to me that you two get along."

"She's fiercely protective of you; so am I. We'll get along just fine."

Rinsing the final dish, Samson shut the water off and wiped his hands on a towel, then turned to face me with his arms crossed. "I can protect myself just fine."

"Never said you couldn't."

"And I'll protect you, too."

"I appreciate that."

"No feminist rant?"

Smiling, I set the towel aside and placed my palms against his crossed forearms. "In my life, I've always been alone. I survived by being vigilant, by not forming relationships. It was lonely, but I endured. I once heard a saying about relationships—that they are just two people taking turns being strong so the other can break down. You can have two strong people at the same time but not two weak. Me, I've never been weak. I couldn't afford to be. To have someone who is willing and able to take on some of that burden? A partner? It's a gift I never thought I'd receive."

"Take a walk with me."

His change of topic threw me. "What? Where?"

"It might be easier if I show you."

Excusing myself, I went into my room and pulled on cotton pants, a t-shirt, and hiking boots. What a difference twenty-four hours made; at this time yesterday, I'd been certain I could walk away from Samson. Now, both of our secrets had been laid bare.

Perhaps not all secrets. I followed Samson out the door and through town, emerging quickly into the vast desert surrounding the reservation. We left civilization and found a thin path that wound through the foothills of White Mountain. It was the same path Frances and I had taken to find our training ground. Samson stayed unusually quiet as he led the way, glancing over every now and again with a reassuring smile and to check that I was still with him.

I didn't ask any questions, knowing it would be useless to do so. Wherever Samson was taking me was obviously important, and it had my curiosity piqued.

We walked for the better part of an hour, the hot desert sun not affecting either of us as much as it should have. Samson had been born and raised here; the desert was in his blood. As for me—well, Elementals weren't really susceptible to weather extremes.

When we reached the small valley between hills where Frances and I had practiced spells two nights ago, Samson turned directly north and brought me deeper into the hills. White Mountain rose before us, one of four the Apache people believed were sacred. I realized this was where the strange pull I'd felt had come from. There was more to this mountain than met the eye.

Samson looked back at me and offered his hand. Taking it, I watched with trepidation as he placed his other palm against a stone face. The seemingly solid wall rippled and cleared until I could see an entrance to a cave.

"What—" I began to ask, but Samson cut me off with a shake of his head.

"We're almost there," he promised, then stepped inside the darkened interior of the mountain.

I followed, trusting that he wasn't leading me to a human sacrificial altar or something equally morbid. We traveled through a long, narrow passageway until, finally, the space opened to a sight that took my breath away.

Samson and I remained at the entrance as I stared, at a complete loss for words. Yes, there were certainly secrets hidden in these hills.

"This is my family's legacy," Samson said quietly. "You are the first non-blood to be granted entrance."

Sparkling stones embedded in the ceiling and walls lit the space as bright as the day outside. Nearly every available inch of wall space had been covered in drawings; some stick-figured and crude, others incredibly detailed.

In the exact center of the room, rising from the ground itself, stood a stone well with water brimming to the top. Scattered around the room were stone pedestals with various objects, ancient and precious. The air itself hummed with power.

Turning to Samson, I attempted to form my jumbled thoughts into a coherent question. Finally, I said, "I'm going to need more explanation than that."

He nodded, his disarming smile helping to settle my nerves. "Come, let's start here." He led me by our still connected hands, pausing at the first of the cave drawings. A woman rose out of the peak of a mountain, her arms spread to encompass two infant boys. "This is the story of the White Painted Woman. It is said she birthed these two boys—Child of Water and Killer of Enemies. From them, our people were born."

Looking closer, I recognized universal symbols for air, earth, fire, and water. Though many cultures believed in celebrating the four elements, something about them drew me closer. With a delicate finger, I reached out, skimming just above the drawing. There was some kind of magic at work here—a preservation spell, perhaps?

"You can feel it, can't you?" Samson asked softly, watching me closely. "The story continues here, a time of prosperity and happiness. The two boys were raised as mortal but were looked upon as gods. They had immense power and control over the elements."

Sucking in a breath, I examined the next drawing carefully. It showed two older boys—one wielding fire while the other created a storm. The next depiction left me breathless once again. The two boys—teenagers now—were in transition from man to wolf.

"It is said they also had the power to transform into our wolf-brothers," Samson continued, placing one hand over the half-transformed young men. Then, he moved his palm higher to encompass two eagles in the sky. "Or to take on the form of the wise eagle."

"Samson…" I began but wasn't sure exactly what to say. What he was showing me was undeniable. His ancestors were, without a doubt, Elementals. "Do you believe this is true?"

His eyes met mine, something unrecognizable shining in them. "I do. And more than that, I know you do, too."

Shutting my mouth, I swallowed hard but found myself unable to lie. Nodding, I said, "I do. They are called Elementals." With a deep breath, I laid myself on the line. "And I'm one, too."

Chapter 7

There were several beats of silence. I'd just laid myself on the line; though I'd hinted at what I was, I had yet to say it out loud. I waited to be judged, admonished. But, to my surprise, Samson only grinned. "I had a feeling after our conversation last night. That's why I knew you would be allowed in here. The spirits recognize you for who you are."

"And you can just accept me, just like that?" I asked with a quiver in my voice.

"Of course," he said, his expression turning serious. "Lani, I've been told the old stories my whole life. I've had dreams of you my whole life. There's no logical explanation for that. The truth is, I've been in love with you since before I knew what love was."

His words floored me. Every nerve ending tingled, my heart on the verge of bursting.

Samson stepped closer, clasping both of his hands around mine. His eyes seared into me, peering into my very soul. "I know we've just met, but I know with every fiber of my being that we are meant to be together. You are my dream girl, Lani."

His head dipped toward mine, and I was helpless to do anything but remain there, rooted to the spot. He moved slow, giving me plenty of opportunity to back away, to speak, but I couldn't.

Because he was my mate, whether I was ready or not.

Our lips met with the softest pressure, and my eyes slipped closed. He moved again, coaxing them to part. His arms wrapped around my waist, and I pressed myself into him, grabbing onto his shoulders while the world around us blurred and spun.

A cool wind wrapped around us, fusing us together. Soft whispers reached my ears, speaking of their approval and a world beyond.

Samson and I broke our embrace with a gasp, our eyes wide in shock. Neither of us moved or spoke as the voices quieted with the wind. With his arms still wrapped around me, Samson disturbed the silence with awe. "Those were the voices of my ancestors."

"Yes, I believe they were," I murmured back, dazed from discovering Samson's family's past, being contacted by spirits, and, not least, his kiss.

"They approve," he said with a smile. I let out a low chuckle as he took a small step back. "Look, about what I said—I meant it, but I realize you may not feel the same. After all, you didn't spend your life dreaming of me. Did you?"

Laughing again, I shook my head. "No, but then, I don't sleep much."

He paused before answering, "Okay, we'll get back to that. What I mean to say is—I don't want you to feel any pressure here."

Letting out a sigh, I took a healthy step away. It was time to come clean. "Samson, for Elementals, there is only one matching soul for each of us. Some go for many years without ever finding that person—some meet them right away. We call this person our mate. They are our soulmate, our other half." His eyebrows knit as he processed this information, but before he could speak, I barged on. "From the moment we met, I knew you were my mate."

"Really?" he asked, his face instantly brightening.

"Yes," I said, holding up a hand to stall any further questions. "But I told myself I would stay away from you for your own good."

"Fat lot of good that did you, huh?" he said with a wink, attempting to lighten the mood.

Though my lips tipped up in the semblance of a smile, I turned away, my arms crossed over my stomach. "The thing is, I have no idea who I am. I don't remember my past, who my family is. For a long time, I remained alone, assuming the worst of every creature like me that I came across. I've killed, Samson."

"You've survived," he corrected gently.

"The point is, I could never be good enough for you. How can I be the other half of your soul when I don't even know who I am?"

There was absolute silence as I stared at the ground, waiting for Samson to condemn me. His light touch against my arms had me looking up into the warm brown of his eyes.

"Your past is not who you are," he said quietly but with utter conviction. "I know who you are. I've seen it. You risk your life to save others. You are strong, caring, and fierce. Maybe we'll find your family, maybe we won't—but that doesn't matter to me. Only you do."

The warmth in my chest began to spread at his words, and I gave in to my needs by collapsing against him, resting my cheek alongside his chest while his arms tightened around my waist. "Thank you. I'll never deserve you, Samson Blackfoot...but I'd like to try."

"Silly, beautiful woman. You don't have to try," Samson said with a smile. We stood like that, each finding comfort in the other for a long time. Eventually, he asked, "Would you like to hear the rest of the stories?"

Nodding, I stepped away again, reaching up to brush a stray strand of hair from his face. "Very much so."

He led me through each drawing, speaking of his family's past. When we reached a story about the last of the Elementals—twin sisters—I traced a hand over the depiction on the wall.

"Eagle Eye and Silver Moon," Samson supplied. "The powerful gene passed on from the twin boys began to water down. These sisters were the last of their kind—the last of the Elementals. It was said Eagle Eye could see the future. She married a man from another tribe and left to live with him. No one knows what happened to her. Silver Moon was a powerful medicine woman who married within our own tribe. Her gift of healing was passed down mother to daughter until a famous medicine woman—Lozan."

"That's incredible," I said, then took in the features of the women again. They looked awfully familiar. "You said Eagle Eye saw the future. You don't know if she had a son?"

Samson looked at me sharply. "It's not in our stories."

"I've told you about Jade and Talon. Talon is an Elemental; he told me he was part of the Apache people. That's how I came to be here. His mother was a foreseer. They lived off the land—just Talon, his mother, and his father. His mother was an Elemental, but his father was not. She converted Talon when he became an adult."

Samson's eyes were wide. "There's a very good possibility that's her."

"Talon and Jade are supposed to join me soon. Would it be possible to bring him here?"

"I don't see why not. If he's blood, the cave will allow him entrance. And it would mean we're *really* extended cousins."

At my questioning look, Samson brought me down the line until we came to drawings I recognized. One, the renowned leader Geronimo; the other, the medicine woman, Lozan.

"My father is, and therefore I am, a direct descendant of Geronimo," Samson explained. "There are many stories that say he had supernatural powers. Though he wasn't fully Elemental, I believe he held onto many of the attributes. My mother is, and therefore I am, also a direct descendant of Lozan. So, however many generations back that is, it would make me cousins to this Talon."

"Does that mean your mother has the healing ability?"

"She does, along with my aunt Emilia."

"Twins," I murmured. "Wow, you have a very powerful line. In fact, you are—as is the rest of your family—what we call Gifted. In other words, you carry latent abilities. You can…you could be converted."

"To become like you?"

I nodded mutely. "It is not an easy thing, but it is possible."

"Something to think about. What of Frances? What's his story?"

"You will have to ask him for that; I wouldn't feel right speaking about his past with you. He is an Elemental also, but the rest—it is up to him if he would like to share."

Though I could see him teeming with curiosity, Samson merely nodded. "I can respect that. You're not actually cousins, though, are you?"

"No," I said with a grin. "Not blood-related."

We were near the end of the cave drawings, so I pointed to the well in the center of the room and asked, "What is that?"

"Come see." He took my hand and led the way. We approached the well, a perfectly round opening filled to the brim with calm, clear water. The entire area pulsed even more strongly with power, and I paused a few steps away.

"There is strong magic here."

"You can feel that, too? I shouldn't be surprised. This is called the Divining Pool. It shows visions to the chosen one, who then becomes caretaker of the cave."

I didn't go any closer. Something kept me back, though the power buzzed around me. "It's not time."

Samson gave me a sharp look. "What's not time?"

Shaking my head, I took a step back and then another. "We should go."

Samson and I left the cave together, but we didn't speak about the Divining Pool again. If he had asked me to explain, I'm not sure that I could have. There were times in this life that defied logic and reasoning.

My very existence proved that.

By mutual agreement, we walked back toward town, our conversation switching back to the light and carefree. I found myself relaxing with Samson in a way I'd never thought would be possible. In a matter of days, he'd managed to sneak under my defenses and lodge directly in my heart. Every time he reached out to take my hand, our skin-to-skin contact sent a frizzle of awareness along my veins.

If I focused too long on any of it, I'd begin to hyperventilate. Instead, I took it one step—and one touch—at a time.

We made dinner together and ate el fresco on the same little couch we'd slept on the night before. Frances remained incognito, which I appreciated. I think he needed some time to himself after he'd laid himself on the line the night before. Though I understood how difficult speaking of his past had been, I was glad he'd trusted me enough to share. It not only helped me understand him better but holding something like that inside couldn't have been healthy for him.

Perhaps, if he'd had a friend when he'd been ten, he wouldn't have turned to the darkness. And his sister....

I wondered about her. He hadn't found her body that night, only the older boy's. Could she have survived? It wasn't something I wanted to bring up with him. Hope could be a wonderful thing, but false hope, devastating. After so many years, it would be important to tread carefully.

"What are you thinking about?" Samson asked. We were sitting together still, watching as the sun sank and the stars appeared.

"Frances. I worry for him."

"How so?"

"You wouldn't know it by looking at him, but he holds a lot of guilt inside. I was wondering if there's a way to help him."

"If there's a way, you know you can count on me."

Looking up at him, I instantly got sucked into his dark gaze. Instead of answering, I closed the distance between us. Tasted his soft lips with my own. "Thank you."

"Anytime." He sighed and looked up at the waning moon. "It's getting late."

"We both have work tomorrow."

"I don't want to leave you."

Smiling, I rested my head against his shoulder. "Will you have dinner with me tomorrow?"

"I would love to." Tipping my chin up with two fingers, he looked deep into my eyes before kissing me softly. My whole world tilted, swirled. With a groan, he stood and helped me to my feet. We walked around to the front door, where he wrapped his arms around my back. "It feels weird to leave you."

"We'll see each other tomorrow."

"That's a long time from now," he said, pressing his lips to mine again. My head tipped back as his tongue swept across the seam of my lips and coaxed them open. His arms tightened until I was pressed firmly against his hard length. A soft sigh strangled in my throat, and he lifted his head with a long-suffering groan. "You better go inside now, or I'll never leave."

Part of me wanted to yank him back, to force him to finish what he'd started. My body was on fire in a way that was new and terrifying.

In a way that only my mate could make me feel. My fingers itched to grab him and not let go. Instead, I backed away, pressing them to my mouth. Holding the taste and feel of him there. "Goodnight, Samson."

"Goodnight, Lani."

I stepped inside, closed the door slowly, and let out a happy sigh. When I turned, I found Frances standing, staring, his arms crossed and a frown on his face. "About time you got done making out with your boyfriend."

"You look like a disapproving father."

"I feel like one." He relaxed his arms and studied me. "Are you happy?"

"Yes. I—I had no idea. What it was like with a mate. I didn't think I'd ever have one."

"You deserve every happiness in the world, Lani. God knows you've earned it."

His words warmed me, but I didn't miss the melancholy edge to them. He wanted this, too. "She's out there, you know. Your mate. I feel it in my bones."

"I hope you're right."

Deciding we both needed a distraction—me from finding Samson and ripping his clothes off and Frances from his hopelessness—I said, "Let's go practice tonight."

His expression instantly lightened. "Cool. I've been working on some things I'd like to show you."

"I'm all in," I said, opening the door and shielding us from view. "Race you."

We both transformed into hawks, letting the wind take us high and deep into the desert. We went back to the same training spot, though I now knew that what I'd felt that first night had been the cave calling to me. I didn't tell Frances about it—not yet. It didn't feel like my secret to share.

We practiced hard. Frances created a kind of obstacle course, forcing me to shift from leopard to human to eagle, clothing and unclothing myself in the process. My transitions weren't as smooth as I'd like, but I enjoyed the exercise. Not just the physicalness of it but the mental and magical aspects as well. I'd never thought to practice things quite like this.

I'd always just survived.

Frances and I raced, and by the third round, I beat him by a millisecond. At that, I decided we'd earned a break. Sipping from a water bottle, I stretched out on the hard ground and grinned. "This is fun."

"It is. It's been a long time since I've done anything like this."

"I'm embarrassed to say I never thought to hone my skills this way. I should have."

"You survived. At times, that's no easy feat."

Setting the water bottle down, I broached the subject that had been running through my mind earlier. "Have you been back to Malta? Since the attack?"

He immediately shuttered off. "No."

"Have you thought about it?"

For a long moment, he remained silent, then let out a sigh. "Yes. More so recently. For a long time, I was too afraid. Then, I was so focused on the dark power I could harness. But now—"

"If you ever decide to go, I will accompany you. I'm sure Samson would, too. As would Jade and Talon. You wouldn't be alone, Frances."

He nodded, though he refused to meet my gaze. "Thank you. All right, that's a long enough break. Onto the hard stuff."

Chapter 8

Frances and I arrived home early enough to get ready for work. We both showered off the night and then I fixed breakfast—including a bag of blood for each of us—before gathering my things for the office. As we were about to leave, there was a knock on the door.

Before opening it, I knew it was Samson. He grinned wide and held out two to-go cups of coffee. "Black for you, cream for Frances."

"Thank you," I said, accepting the coffee and the kiss.

"I also came to offer Frances a ride to the job site. That way, you don't have to go out of your way."

"It's not much out of the way, but I'm sure he'll appreciate it."

Frances came out with his new work boots laced and his orange vest slung over his arm. "Hey, man. You brought me coffee?"

"I did. And I'll even let you hitch a ride. Ready to go?"

"Sure. See you later, Lani."

Samson winked, pulled me in for another kiss, and whispered in my ear, "Until tonight."

Laughing, I shoved him out the door, waving as they drove away. Grabbing my things, I got in the truck and headed into Tularosa. After greeting Dave with a bright smile, I got to work. Before lunch, I'd managed to make decent headway on the backlog of paperwork. Juan came in and dropped off the previous week's timecards as I heated up leftovers in the ancient microwave.

"How did it go with MSHA?"

"They investigated, interviewed all the guys. There won't be any fines, thank God. It's a miracle no one got injured."

Keeping a straight face, I nodded. "We can be grateful for that much."

"Frances is working out well. None of us believed he'd make it a day. He's a tough little bugger, isn't he?"

"You have no idea."

Once Juan left, I ate my meal and got back to work. Dave was an easy office companion—besides his phone constantly ringing, he kept to himself. Emanuel checked in a couple of times, but otherwise, he preferred to be out in the field. I appreciated being left to my own devices.

As the workday neared an end, I sent a quick message to Jade to let her know Frances and I were settling in and had found a group of Gifted that could very well be related to Talon. I didn't mention the fact that Samson was my mate—that wasn't something to be discussed over text. I asked her to get back to me when she had time.

When I packed up for the day, I felt an unusual tingling in the pit of my stomach. For a moment, I pressed my hand there, wondering what could be wrong. Then I realized it was nerves. I would be going home and getting ready for a date. I was *nervous*.

Never mind that I'd spent the better part of the last two days with Samson.

"Lani? You okay?" Dave asked.

Turning to him with half a laugh, I shook my head in sheer amazement. "I'm nervous."

"About what?"

"I have a date tonight, and I'm nervous."

Dave didn't seem to understand the bafflement behind my revelation, but his eyes crinkled with a smile. "Lucky guy. Anyone I know?"

"Samson Blackfoot."

"Good guy. The best, really. Why are you nervous?"

I sat down on the edge of the desk, eyes wide as I came to grips with what was going on inside me. "I haven't dated much."

"Really? Smart, beautiful girl like you?" When I raised an eyebrow, Dave held out his hands. "Pure observation. I'm old enough to be your father, at least."

Not strictly true, but I'd let him slide. "You could say I'm...picky."

"As you should be. No one should settle. But with Samson, I don't think you would be."

"No, I don't think I would be."

"Then what's the problem?"

Melancholy washed through me. "What if I'm not good enough for him?"

Dave stood and leaned against the desk facing me. His hands clasped as he studied me, and I appreciated that he took my question seriously. Most wouldn't. "I think the fact that you're asking that question means you are. I don't know what happened to make you feel down on yourself, but the fact that you're concerned about something like that—especially so early on—means to me that you'll do everything in your power to live up to your full potential. To be the person you're meant to be."

"That was very wise, Dave."

He grinned. "I have my moments. Now get out of here. Have fun on your date."

I took Dave's advice to heart. Samson deserved the best part of me—the part that remained cloaked in shadow. The journey to finding my family and recover my memories was far from over. But I wouldn't stop living in the meantime. Finding a mate was a gift, ready or not. It was time I acted that way.

Samson brought Frances home and promised he'd be back shortly. After a day at the mine, he was caked in dirt and grime, so he wanted to go home and shower before our dinner date. I kept myself busy making the meal and setting the scene. Frances took his plate and disappeared into his room—I knew if he wanted to go out and do something, he'd use the window.

When Samson returned, he wore dark jeans and a simple black tee. His lean body filled them out nicely, and my mouth began to water—but not for the food I'd prepared.

As soon as I answered the door, he wrapped me up in a savage embrace and kissed me senselessly. I forgot my name and all my insecurities—and the food starting to burn on the stove.

Pulling away, gasping for air, I looked up at him in a daze. "Hello to you, too."

"I missed you all day," Samson said, bending to kiss along my collarbone. "You smell good."

"It's probably the enchiladas."

His head popped up. "Enchiladas?"

"With refried beans on the side, which I believe are burning because you distracted me. Come in, sit. Would you like something to drink?"

"Water's fine. Smells spicy."

"That they are. Hope you can handle it."

"I have no doubts."

He followed me into the kitchen, taking out plates and utensils while I took the beans off the heat and pulled the pan from the oven. Once I plated the food, Samson brought it all to the small table where I'd arranged the bouquet of flowers he'd brought along with a few candles.

Taking a bite, Samson nodded approvingly. "These are amazing and the perfect amount of heat."

"Glad you like them. How was work?"

He told me about his day, including a few more details on the MSHA visit than Juan had given. I told him about mine, how accomplished I felt at the end of it. The only thing I left out was my bout of nerves and Dave's pep talk.

There were some things he didn't need to know.

We took two glasses of wine outside and settled in our little loveseat. Sunset had always been my favorite time of day, and the desert sky didn't disappoint. Brilliant streaks of dark pink and orange filled the horizon even as the first stars made themselves known.

"It's so beautiful here," I said.

Samson's gaze switched to my face. His palm cupped my cheek, urging me to look at him. "It sure is."

Warmth spread through me at his words and then ignited when his lips touched mine. I sank into the kiss, letting the rest of the world fall away until I could only feel. A wild part of me wanted to straddle Samson right there, right then, and damn the consequences.

Instead, I pulled back. "Samson, there's something we should talk about."

"Uh oh," he said. "Nothing good starts with those words."

"Oh, no, nothing bad. Not really. Um...." I was totally messing this up. Mortifying spots of color settled on my cheeks. Now I was blushing? I barely recognized the woman sitting here in the moonlight with a man. I was so far out of my milieu I needed a passport. "It's just that...I've never done...this."

Samson stared at me before breaking into a smile. "Neither have I."

"But you're so good at it," I said before I could sensor myself.

He chuckled and cupped my cheeks with his palms. "And here I was thinking it was all you."

"I guess we're just good together," I said, feeling a bit breathless. "Believe me when I say I want this—I want you. But I'm not sure I'm fully ready yet."

"Lani, there's no rush on anything. I mean it. We can take as long as you need."

A weight I hadn't realized had been sitting on my chest lifted. Resting my head against his shoulder, I took a deep breath of the night and found solace in the arms of my mate.

∞　∞　∞

THE ROUTINE OF WORK, SPENDING time with Samson, and practicing with Frances was easy to fall into. I hadn't heard back from Jade, either, but knew she had her hands full with the amnestic Elemental and newly converted shadowmen.

Samson brought me out to dinner on Tuesday but decided to try his hand at grilling on Wednesday night. He rented a room from Josiah and Tayen. The newlyweds decided to join us for dinner—the men grilled while I helped Tayen chop a salad.

She poured a glass of wine for each of us. I took a sip and smiled. "I like how you cook."

"Nothing like a glass of wine after a long day. So, tell me, how is everything going with you and Samson? You seem to be spending a lot of time together."

"We are. He surprised me."

"A good surprise?"

"A wonderful surprise."

Her eyes twinkled as she smiled. I liked Tayen. She had an easy grace and flawless style that I envied. Then she took my hand, and her expression went stoic, then blank. I felt a warm tingling in my palm, and I realized she had the gift of sight.

When I tried to pull back, she tightened her grip beyond human means. Her eyes took on a misty quality, and she spoke in a disembodied voice. "By the light of the moon, they come. With haze of red and magicks yet known. Beware the devil inside, for he is stronger by far. You cannot do this alone."

Tayen stepped back, blinked several times. Offered me half a smile. "Sorry. Blanked out for a minute there. What were we talking about?"

Fear tripped down my spine. "I have to go."

Before she could protest, I ran outside and straight into Samson. He grabbed my arms to steady me before taking in the look on my face. "What is it? What's wrong?"

"I—I don't know."

He sent Josiah a glance, then led me into a private section of the backyard. "It's okay, I'm here. Just talk to me."

"Do you feel that?" I rubbed my arms, shot hard glances around. I didn't understand what had just happened or what I felt now, but I knew everything was about to change. "Something is calling me."

Samson looked concerned, but he stilled, quieted. Listened hard. "I don't hear anything."

Moving away from him, I began to walk. The walk turned into a run, Samson hot on my heels. In the back of my head, I knew I had to keep it to a human pace in order for him to keep up, but I was having a difficult time restricting myself. Something tugged at me, pulled me relentlessly closer.

When we found ourselves past the rise of the northern hills, I paused, searching my surroundings. I knew exactly where I was being led. Part of me always knew.

"The cave," I whispered. Samson caught me, out of breath from our unexpected jaunt.

"The cave? You think it's calling you?"

Pressing a hand against my heart, I nodded, staring at the opening. Without another word, I stepped closer and placed my palm against the faux wall. It rippled, opened. I stepped through with Samson at my back. Dread filled me, but not from the cave itself. Somehow, I knew whatever it wanted to tell me wouldn't be good.

As if in a trance, I moved forward, directly for the Divining Pool. Samson's palm rested against my lower back, my anchor in this strange storm of sensations. He didn't utter a word, understanding this was something I needed to do. Cautiously approaching the pool, I lifted my hands, felt the power there. Tested it. The well drew me closer. It was time.

I stepped up on the ledge and looked down into the crystal-clear waters. For a long, drawn-out moment, nothing happened. My own face reflected back at me—eyes large with concern, long hair flowing over my shoulders.

The water rippled, turned opaque. I bent closer, though not of my own will. And then I was falling.

When I opened my eyes, I blinked several times to clear away the haze of a dream. No, not a dream. A vision.

In the dark of night, the heat of day remained. It hung heavy above the sandy earth, broken up only by the occasional Joshua tree and other spindly flora of the desert.

The moon glowed dimly in the sky as if masked by a thick layer of haze. Stumbling forward, I searched urgently, feverishly, for something just out of reach. Dread built in my limbs and slowed my steps. Glancing down at my tattered, blood-streaked clothes, I realized dread wasn't the only thing slowing me down. I'd been injured.

Suddenly, the haze cleared, and a woman stood before me. Her wide, amber eyes latched onto me with such urgency I found myself rooted to the spot.

"What is it?" she called out. "Who are you?"

Unable to speak, I managed to mouth the words before collapsing to the ground. "Help me."

Coming back into the cavern with a gasp, I stumbled back, Samson catching me before hitting the ground with my butt. Samson eased us to the earth, my name on his lips as he checked for injuries. "Lani! What happened? Are you all right?"

Giving my head a few hard shakes, I took a moment to breathe. Just to breathe. "I'm—I'm not sure."

"What did you see?"

Before I could answer, great rumbles shook the earth. Rock and debris tumbled from the walls as we struggled to stand. Without thinking, I grabbed Samson and hovered above the ground as it upheaved violently beneath us.

Before I could consider the repercussions, I opened our mental link and called out to him on our private path. *Hold on.*

Though my voice inside his head must have startled him, he didn't question it, just wrapped his arms around my waist as I called upon the wind to keep us above the ground. The small opening we'd walked through was being covered quickly as more and larger rocks and boulders began to fall.

Spirit of wind, I call to you. Protect me and my mate as we fly through. Shield of energy, shield of light. Create this barrier from my might!

We had no time left. Charging toward the diminishing exit, I took the brunt of falling debris against my shield. Samson held tight and still as we burst from the cave and entered a world gone mad.

We were met with red-hued skies and murky, hazy air. All around us, the earth had shifted as if throwing a childish fit. I could see no safe place to land. Samson stared around us in shock. Neither of us understood what had just happened.

"My family," he finally managed to say. "We need to get to my family."

"Do you trust me?" I asked.

His eyes met mine, and after the briefest of hesitations, he nodded. Closing my eyes to concentrate as the world around us crumbled to pieces, I pulled in my very essence until I shimmered as the air itself, then transformed into a creature large enough to carry the weight of my mate.

Less than a second later, I spread my wings and grasped Samson in my talons, using the animal's natural speed to make our way back to his family. With the acute senses of the eagle, I could hear Samson gasping for breath.

Are you all right?

At first, he didn't answer. Nerves wound tight as the prospect of Samson turning against me hit full force. All of this was too much for a human. I should have known better. I should have disappeared, run as soon as I'd known him to be my mate. Now, I would have to deal with the consequences. I steeled myself against his rejection as I felt the first flutters of a response in my mind.

I'm fine. Terrified for my family, but.... He seemed hesitant to finish his thought.

What is it?

This is so cool. You are an amazing woman, Lani.

His reply took me by surprise, to say the least. I dipped in our flight, nearly lost my grip as my heart raced. He thought I was amazing? *I promise we'll go flying under less stressful circumstances.*

I felt a wealth of emotion flood our connection. *How are we speaking this way?*

Mates are able to speak telepathically.

You didn't tell me sooner?

I didn't want to frighten you. Now, soaring above the land his family had called home for generations, clutching him in the eagle's powerful grip, I realized what a ridiculous thought that had been. *Any more than necessary, I suppose.*

We approached his parents' house as the quakes began to cease. Setting Samson lightly on his feet, I landed beside him and scanned the area with all my senses. "They're inside," I said. "Frightened but safe."

Obvious relief washed over his features as he ran inside. I wanted to join him, but I had to scout the area. *Stay inside. I'll be right back.*

What? Where are you going? Let me come with you!

In the blink of an eye, I shimmered and transformed into my most comfortable form—the leopard. Though wildly out of place in this desert environment, the cat was fast and agile. I ran toward the horizon because I wanted to see how far this strange phenomenon went. Paws padded against the ground in a soothing rhythm, easily navigating the rough terrain.

I'm okay, Samson. I'll be back soon, I promise. Please stay with your family.

He didn't reply, though I could feel his fear. Another voice spoke into my mind—now that I had a comparison to make, I realized how vastly different it felt to have a mate connection over speaking to animals. Or, in this case, Elementals in animal form.

Any idea what's going on? Frances asked.

Not exactly, but I know how it started. Checking the barrier now.

I'll join you.

Giving him my direction, I was soon joined by a snow leopard, Frances' favored animal. Though the smallest of the large cats, leopards are the most agile and strong for their size, which comes in handy when racing over uneven ground with uprooted trees and other obstacles.

We raced together using our supernatural speed, slowing as the haze thickened. From there, I crept slowly forward, testing the boundary of magic that seemed to have sprung up out of nowhere.

It looks as if there is a dome over the entire reservation.

Stay here. I'm going to see if I can penetrate it.

Though I didn't want to, I remained in the thick haze. One of us had to keep a lookout.

I can see blue skies beyond, but the air feels too thick to pass. After a brief pause, I heard a grunt of pain. When I began to rush toward him, Frances stopped me. *There's strong magic at work here. It won't let me pass.*

Like a spell? Think you can unravel it?

Maybe. He appeared from the thick haze and looked directly at me. *It will take me some time. I've never seen the likes of this before.*

All right. We need to make sure everyone's safe and put some kind of emergency protocol in place. And then we'll come back here, try to figure out the problem and if we can break it.

As we began to run back, Frances asked, *What started this?*

Before I could respond, an ear-splitting howl filled the air. Without needing to discuss it, we both turned in the direction of the wounded animal.

We came upon a home devastated by the unusual quake. To my shock, three wolves were gripping crumbled timber in their mouths and tossing it aside. A low, plaintive cry rose up from beneath the wreckage—a fourth wolf.

Frances and I slowed to survey the scene. These were no ordinary wolves, and I wanted to be careful with how we approached this. With my ability to speak to animals, I'd always been able to coexist peacefully when I came across even the most ferocious in the wild.

The three massive heads turned toward us as we neared, low growls emanating from their throats. I kept my posture relaxed as I reached out to reassure them that we were friendly. Using soothing images more than actual words, I let them know we wanted to help.

Calm. It's all right. We've come to help. Calm.

The wolves straightened, and the growling ceased. *Who are you?*

The shock of getting a reply shouldn't have been so great. What were the odds of four wolves in the desert working together? About the same as two leopards.

My name is Lani Brown. Who are you?

Thank goodness. Lani. It's Atienn. Nova's trapped; we're trying to get her.

That meant the other two wolves were Chayton and Tala. I'd never heard of humans—even Gifted humans—being able to shift, but that would have to be examined later. I quickly shifted into human form, using my newfound tricks Frances had taught me to fashion cotton pants and a shirt. Simultaneously, I brought Frances up to speed.

He shifted within a split second, and between the two of us, we were able to harness enough magic to lift the rubble up and away from the injured wolf. The three that had been so frantically digging scooted away, and if wolves could look shocked, they did.

Where is your mom? I asked telepathically to Atienn.

We don't know. This is—was their home. We were coming to make sure they were all right, but they weren't home.

"Frances, bring Nova to Neveah. She's home. You three, find the rest of your family and meet us at the Blackfoots'."

Tala whined, so I looked directly at her. "She will be fine. We'll make sure of it." As I spoke, Frances knelt at Nova's side. I could hear him speaking softly before lifting her easily into his arms. Then, before our sights, he disappeared. "Go, now. As long as you're in wolf form, I can keep you updated, and you can reach out to me."

They didn't question this. The boys instantly turned and ran off, Tala hesitating just a moment more. I knew how close the girls were—all four of them, really—and understood it took a lot of willpower to leave Nova in pain.

Samson, Frances is on his way with Nova. She's injured; your mom needs to help her. Atienn, Chayton, and Tala are looking for Emilia.

I could sense his panic, but after several seconds, he got back to me. *Gathering supplies now. They've just arrived. Are you okay?*

I am. I'm going to see if there are any others injured, and then I'll join you.

Be safe.

Without another word, I shimmered and transformed back into an eagle. I needed a bird's eye view, and I needed to see the extent of the barrier surrounding us. First, I flew as high as I was able to see if I could penetrate the spell from the air. No luck.

I hit the barrier, and pain blossomed in my head. I began to free fall. Spreading my wings out to catch the wind, I soared higher but just under the thickest part of the haze. Atienn updated me when they found their mom, and Samson let me know as each family member arrived.

For now, I flew over the houses, keeping a sharp eye and close ear on anyone else who might be trapped. Once that was done, I made my way back to the Blackfoots'. Landing on bare feet and wearing my simple clothing fashioned from the earth, I strode inside to find Samson and his family all staring despondently. The house still stood intact, though frames had fallen off the walls and smaller objects had broken in the strange upheaval.

Electricity was out. Someone had lit enough candles to make up for the lack of light. Forcing confidence into my voice, I asked, "Everyone is all right?"

"Yes," Samson's dad, Santiago, answered. "Nova will need some time, but Neveah and Emilia are with her now. So are Tala and Frances."

Samson enveloped me in his arms, his nose pushing its way through my hair to inhale my scent. "Thank goodness you're all right. What happened?"

"I'm not sure, but I think we all need to talk."

Chapter 9

All eyes were on me. I briefly glanced at the two shifters in the room, took a deep breath, then spoke again. "It seems most in the town were unharmed. I did a quick sweep and didn't see anything that needed immediate attention."

"What are you?" Chayton burst out, which earned a backhanded slap on his arm from his father, Domingo.

"I am an Elemental. Based on what I've seen today, I have a feeling none of this will shock any of you."

Samson clasped my hand. Presented a united front to his family. "I brought Lani to the cave."

"You did what?" Raven exclaimed. "No outsider has ever been admitted entrance to the cave!"

"She's not an outsider," Samson said. "She's my mate."

Jaws dropped at his words. Raven recovered first. "What the hell's a mate?"

"And what the hell is an Elemental?" Atienn pitched in.

"This is a long story, and I'll be happy to answer any and all of your questions. Just so you have an idea, your ancient stories—the twins who created your people—they were like me. You all still carry the gene. That's why you two can shift"—I gestured toward Atienn and Chayton—"and I'm sure there're more. To answer your question, Raven, for Elementals, there is only one other person—a soulmate if you will—for each of us. Samson is mine."

"But what—"

"We have more important things to discuss right now," Santiago interrupted Raven's next question. "All electricity and phones have been cut off."

"We need to organize all those in town. Is there a central location where we can gather everyone together? Something with a generator?" I asked, looking at the elder generation in the room.

Viktor nodded. "Our community center should hold all of us, and it has a backup generator. We need to sort out food and shelter, tend to any injured."

Neveah appeared from upstairs, along with Frances. "Nova will be fine. She's resting and needs some time to heal. Luckily, her wolf genes will speed along that process."

I had a feeling Frances had also donated some blood. He'd become attached to the twins in the short time we'd been there.

"Thank you, Neveah," Domingo said. "I would like to check on my daughter. Why don't you all decide our course of action, and I will be willing to do whatever is necessary."

Viktor and Santiago nodded their agreement while Neveah took her place beside Santiago. He wrapped an arm around his wife and looked at me. "Why don't you tell us what happened?"

"We went to the cave, as Samson said. He told me of your histories, the original twin boys, Child of Water and Killer of Enemies. I believe they were Elementals—like me." I paused here, but when no one questioned my conclusion, I continued. "The first time we went, I approached the Divining Pool but felt it wasn't time. Today, I felt pulled back to the cave, back to the well. It showed me a vision."

"The Divining Pool spoke to you?" Santiago asked.

"It did, though I don't understand what I saw. It was nighttime and still hot. I walked through the desert—no homes or other buildings in sight—and I was searching for something. My clothes were in shreds, and there was blood...so much blood. Just as I was about to give up, a woman appeared. I'd never seen her before; she had beautiful, unusual amber eyes and dark hair streaked with red. She said, 'What is it? Who are you?' I said, 'Help me,' then collapsed."

"Viktor? Any ideas?" Santiago asked.

I realized the whole room looked at the older man, and I wondered what his connection to this could be. His gaze met mine, held steady. "It doesn't bode well. It seems we need to find this woman—she wasn't one of our tribe?"

"No, I don't believe so. I have friends in California who have been trying to join me here, but with no way to reach them, we can't count on their help, either. Once they realize they can't reach me by phone, I'm sure they'll come investigate. This leads us to the next problem—the barrier. Frances tried to breach it earlier without luck."

Domingo reappeared then, calmer at having seen his daughter on the mend.

"My plan is to go back and see if I can find a weak point," Frances told everyone. "Before we do anything, though, I think it's time we all came clean. I'll start. I'm also an Elemental with a knack for spells. Who's next?"

Stifling a grin at his to-the-point attitude, I happily joined in. "I'm able to speak with animals—or with an Elemental in animal form. And, as it turns out, Gifted in animal form."

Atienn and Chayton smiled broadly at that. "You all know what we can do, along with Tala and Nova. Wolf's out of the bag."

"My sister and I are able to heal," Neveah piped up.

Niko, who sat on the sofa hugging her girls, spoke next. "I have an affinity for growing things. Kateri is able to see auras, Koko is an empath, and Kaiah...it's not quite mind reading, but that might be the easiest way to describe it."

Surprised, I stared at the youngest of the group, who hid behind her mom's arm. I'd never come across a mind-reader before. "Wow. How about you, Kai?"

She looked at Niko and only answered after a nod of approval. "I can hold an object and see its history."

"Very impressive," I said, then looked to Raven. "What can you do?"

"I can tell when someone is being truthful—and when they're lying."

Samson squeezed my hand, then spoke quietly. "Languages come easily to me. Some call it omnilingualism or aligist. Basically, I can understand and speak any language I hear."

"Good to know," I murmured. Before I could ask anything more about that remarkable ability, Viktor explained his connection to the Divining Pool.

"The eldest of our family has always been charged with being the keeper of the cave. Since I'm a few minutes older than Santiago, that task fell to me," he said with a wink. "I am the only one of the tribe alive today who has seen visions in its waters."

"I'm honored to have been chosen to see," I said, feeling overwhelmed not only by the talent in Samson's family but by their history.

He is also the president of the Tribal Council and technically the chief of our tribe, Samson informed me privately. *Our people don't officially recognize a chief anymore, but it's kind of an unspoken honor.*

Your family is amazing, I sent back to him before speaking aloud. "Domingo, you're the only one who hasn't shared."

He stood, squeezed his wife's shoulder. Looked to his sons with pride. "I will go with Frances to the border."

"Really? What can you do?" Frances asked.

"I'm able to see magic," he said simply. "I can see it around each person in this room. I can see it in the air. And right now, we are quite literally surrounded by a magic darker than anything I've ever seen."

"I've never heard of that." Frances looked to be truly in awe. "I have to enact a spell in order to see the threads of magic. You just see them all the time?"

"I do. It is like learning a new language—the threads turn into words, and I can read them. Once you know the words, you can reverse most anything."

"Huh." Frances turned to me and raised his eyebrows. "Okay, I'll take magic-man here and head back to the boundary."

"We're coming with," Atienn said for himself and his brother. "For added protection."

"All right. Keep me updated," I told them. "We'll work on gathering everyone we can find at the community center. I'd like to do another flyover, see if I can find who or what caused this."

I want to come with you.

It's all right. Your family and the rest of the town need your help. If I see anything, I won't engage without backup. I promise.

"We'll help, too," Nova announced. She hobbled down the stairs with Tala's help. Emilia hovered just behind. "Thank you, Frances and Lani. You saved me."

Frances hurried over to give her a hand down. "You should rest."

"I can move; I'm going to help. So, what's the plan?"

I left the organizing to Santiago and Viktor. As Frances, Domingo, Atienn, and Chayton left, so did I. Samson followed me out, pulling me into his arms and placing a hard kiss on my mouth. "Come back to me in one piece."

"I will," I promised. "Get everyone to safety. That's the most important thing right now."

The rest of his family came outside, taking in the strange red hue in the sky. I nodded at them and wished them luck before pulling myself in and exploding out in the shape of an eagle. I heard the gasps as I spread my wings and caught the wind, soaring quickly up into the sky. It was one thing to see it in the painting on a cave wall, quite another to witness such a transformation in real life.

Starting from their home, I began making gradually larger circles. I spotted a strange encampment deep in the mountains, south of town. Slowing, I approached cautiously, knowing in my gut that whatever—whoever—had caused the quake, the barrier, I'd just found them.

Circling the camp now in continuously smaller loops, I spotted movement on the ground. Men—tall, muscular men. They moved quickly, building and fortifying their settlement. As I moved closer, I stumbled in my flight and nearly tumbled to the earth for the second time that day.

For I was looking at no mere man, not even Elementals or shadowmen. No, these were something different, something much, much worse.

Two long, elegant horns protruded from each of their heads. They weren't just tall and muscular; they were massive. The smallest clocked in at about seven feet with shoulders to match.

Who were they? What were they doing here?

One thing I knew for certain—I couldn't do this alone.

∞ ∞ ∞

THERE WERE ROUGHLY THIRTEEN HUNDRED people living in Mescalero, and by a quick scan, it looked close to that number huddled in the community center. Santiago and Viktor had done a good job putting people in charge of serving food and figuring out sleeping arrangements. Battery-operated lanterns were set throughout the area for light in order to preserve the little power they had.

"It seems to be contained to the reservation. How many injured?" I asked Samson.

"A couple dozen with minor injuries. Luckily, nothing worse. My mom and aunt are helping, along with several nurses and doctors."

"Great. I think the next thing we need to do is to collect anyone in the room who is Gifted and tell them what's going on."

"You think that's wise? It's a lot to handle."

"If your family is any indication, yes, I think they'll be fine. The truth is, I think everyone here could handle it, since they've all heard the stories their whole lives. But let's start with the Gifted because I believe we're going to need all the help we can get. If anyone has an ability that can assist us—"

"Then it's worth it," Samson said with a sigh. "All right. You point them out. Viktor, my dad, and I will gather them together in the next room. Everyone will listen to Viktor and my dad."

After explaining to the older men our plan, Samson and I walked together through the room. Discreetly, I pointed out who I got the Gifted vibe from. Domingo would have been able to identify them even more easily, but he remained busy at the border.

Though I itched to reach out and get an update, I didn't want to distract Atienn or Chayton. They would check in when they had something to say.

All in all, we gathered nearly one hundred people in the conference room. We were stuffed to the gills, but it was our only option for privacy. There were many children who also carried the gene, but we had a mutual agreement to leave them out of this—for as long as we could, at least.

"What's this about, Viktor?" one of the men near the front of the group asked.

Viktor and Santiago had already done their best to calm everyone when they'd first gathered in the community center. Now, we were about to tell them the truth—that there were supernaturals in this world and something worse I had yet to name.

"Everyone, please try to remain calm. I would like to introduce Lani Brown, this remarkable young woman right here. She belongs to Samson, and he to her. Because of that fact alone, she is one of us. Family. She's going to explain some things to you that may seem outrageous, but please, give her your attention and understanding."

Low murmurs spread through the room, which quieted as soon as I began to speak. "Hello, everyone. I'm sorry to meet you in such circumstances, but we need to deal with this threat. The things I'm about to tell you might seem outlandish, but I assure you they are no joke. Later, I'll be happy to answer any and all questions you may have, but for now, I'm going to give you a quick rundown.

"I am what is called an Elemental. Like your stories of the twin boys from which you all hail, I am able to control the natural elements. I am also able to shapeshift, and I have increased strength and speed.

"We have gathered you all into this room because you are what is known as Gifted. That means you carry the gene to become like me.

You have latent abilities that you may not even realize, or—if you're like several Gifted that I've met—you might be able to do certain things that are above and beyond human limitations."

After a stunned silence, the murmurs began again. Holding up my hands, I called for quiet. "Please, I know you'll all have many questions, but time is of the essence. I'm going to ask anyone who does have a special ability to come with us outside. If you don't—or don't feel comfortable helping—then please, rejoin your families."

There were many exchanged looks. Viktor and Santiago watched each face carefully while Samson pulled me aside. "I think we should tell everyone what's going on."

"Everyone?"

He nodded, and I could see he hadn't come to this lightly. "You were right. We have people that can help. Gifted or not, our people would be willing to fight or assist in any way they can. Viktor and my father can talk to the entire group while we go outside with any who volunteer here."

A man approached us before I could respond. He bowed his head respectfully before speaking. "We'd all like to help. Some of us would be more assistance inside—there are some healers and some that can help temper emotions. If this threat is as dangerous as you say, we'll also need fighters to defend our children and elderly and anyone unable to defend themselves."

"What's your name?" I asked, impressed by the quick decision everyone had come to.

"I'm Paco Stone, this is my brother, Kitchi." Paco gestured to the man just behind him, an exact replica of dark, wise eyes and shaggy black hair. "We are direct descendants of the original twins."

"About half the people in this room are closely related to them," Samson said. "The other half related to me."

Josiah approached with Tayen. He clapped Samson on the shoulder and grinned. "We're all related if you go back far enough. And you know I'm in."

Paco smiled proudly, and I realized they were more than relations—they were father and son. Valentina, Josiah's younger sister, joined us. "I'm willing to help, as well."

Wrapping an arm around his daughter's shoulders, Paco looked back at me. Getting over my astonishment, I said, "All right then. Let's start gathering outside, and I'll try to explain what we're dealing with."

Samson spoke with his father and uncle about updating the rest of the tribe, while Paco and Kitchi helped me direct everyone else outside. Only a handful stayed back, and once again, I felt blown away by the bravery in this tight-knit community.

We all gathered together in a loose circle, making it easier for everyone to hear me. Most shot concerned looks at the strange sky, which in turn cast an eerie glow upon everything within the boundary.

When Samson joined my side, I said, "The boundary has formed around Mescalero. We have two men at the border now, working to collapse it, and they can see beyond. Nowhere else seems to be affected. When I scouted earlier, I spotted a strange settlement just south of here." Looking at each determined face around me, I laid it on the line. "There are creatures I've never seen before. They have human shapes, though they seem taller, more muscular. They also have horns protruding from their heads."

"Daemons," someone gasped from the crowd.

"Do your stories speak of creatures like this?" I asked sharply.

Paco answered for them. "The defeat of the twins is said to have been caused by daemons. We always took that to be more figurative than literal..."

"But it appears all of your stories are true," I finished for him. "All right. I think the first thing we need to do is split into categories based on your abilities. If you're able to do something mental, group together over there. If you're able to do something physical, group together over there. If you're not sure, stay in the middle."

After a brief shuffle, the group split into three smaller ones. Only a handful remained in the middle, while there seemed to be a pretty even split otherwise. I turned to the mental abilities first.

"Are any of you able to see magic? Work with spells?" Two hands went up, and I sighed with relief. "I'd like you to join Frances and Domingo at the border. They are working at finding a weakness, a way to take it down. They could use your help."

Hating to interrupt, I first updated Atienn and then asked about their location, letting him know they had two helpers on the way. *Should we return to help fight the threat?*

Continue to protect those at the border, I sent back.

Chayton will meet them and guide them.

"All right, you're heading east," I told the two volunteers. "Chayton, in his wolf form, will be meeting you to show you the way and offer protection. So, you know, don't freak out."

"Follow the wolf," the younger of the two said with a grin. "Got it."

They left, and I looked at the rest of the crowd. "All right, when I point at you, explain your ability as best you can."

I didn't know another way to organize them. Starting with those in the middle, I quickly sorted them into one of the larger groups before continuing with those with mental abilities.

"I can have visions showing me the history of a location," Josiah said as I pointed to him.

"I'm able to have visions of possible futures in a location," Valentina said next. She looked nervous about revealing this, so I smiled encouragingly before moving on.

Tayen had the sight—which I already knew from our interaction in her kitchen—and another had psychometry—able to read an object's history. There were empaths, another seer, and several other abilities I hadn't heard of or that I didn't have a name for.

"Okay. Josiah, I'd like you to come with me when we check out the daemons. I'd also like a seer—or more than one. I'll leave it up to you who would like to join us." Turning away from that group, I went to the next. "I'd like to put together a recon group, so let's do a quick recap of abilities."

We went through the same—I pointed to each, and they spelled out what they could do. There were more shifters, though they didn't have much practice. Some were closely connected to one of the elements, and one person connected easily to all four.

After I'd heard from everyone, I formed four groups. Each had a shifter, so I could communicate as needed. "We're going to need a distraction. Group one, you're going to create it. Group two, you're with me. Once the area clears, we're going in to investigate. Group three, you'll be waiting close by as backup. Group four, you'll be our final line of defense. You'll protect the community center or join us as needed. Everyone understand?"

They all nodded. Nova, still healing, would be my contact in group four. Tala was in group three, and Samson remained firmly by my side for group two.

In group one, I placed all those able to manipulate the elements. I expected to see fires, earthquakes, floods, and tornados— all as a distraction for the daemons. The shifters transformed into their animal forms—all of them wolves, I noted—and I connected to each mentally, so they got comfortable with that type of communication.

Looking up, I managed to spot the moon through the strange haze, shining bright on all but us. This was the first night of the full moon; our magic would be stronger for it.

"All right, group one—my group will escort you to the northwest area of the settlement. From there, we'll continue on to the settlement itself. Once we're in position, I'll notify Lenna." The petite girl nodded, determination set on her face. Her twin brother looked her exact opposite—large, burly, scowling. He'd be coming with me. They were cousins to Josiah and Valentina, also part of my team. "Any questions?"

Everyone shook their heads.

"All right. Let's move out."

Chapter 10

We moved human quick, and though I felt an urgency to hurry them along, I knew stealth was the most important factor here. Group three peeled off at our predesignated spot while I led group one to where I thought they could do the most damage.

"Remember, when I give Lenna the go-ahead, unleash whatever you've got. Just make sure to direct it away from you, then move away fast. The daemons will come, and I don't want you here when they arrive." They all nodded, nerves and fear overshadowed by grim determination. I looked to my group—Samson, by my side. Josiah and Valentina. Elan, Lenna's brother, in his wolf form. Nadie, a seer like Valentina. All ready to defend their people, their land. "Let's go. Quick and quiet and follow my lead. Recon only."

We began to move as one, and I used a spell to make them all light of foot for a boost of speed and for stealth. If they noticed, none of them commented.

When we reached the edge of the strange settlement, I spotted several daemons patrolling the grounds, with several more gathered around a fire—maybe twenty in total. Twenty against over a thousand in the settlement—it seemed like fair odds, but we knew nothing about the strange creatures, about their powers. The fact that their arrival also brought this red haze and effective boundary told me to remain cautious.

Holding up my hand to signal the others to give me a moment, I stretched and expanded my senses. Their voices were muffled as if they'd done some kind of sound suppression. I could see them fine, though, so that either meant they didn't have the power to shield themselves—or they didn't care.

Lenna, we're in position.

She didn't answer. She didn't have to. A streak of fire shot into the air, followed instantly by a plume of smoke. The earth rumbled, shook. The daemons surged into action; the one who seemed to be in charge called out orders and led the search party. A handful remained behind, their attention all diverted.

I led the way down into the valley, using a trick of my own to blur and shield our forms. We moved as one into the encampment. Splitting up might have been doable if any of them had battle experience or elemental powers. As it was, Elan and I were the muscle, and we were determined to keep the rest safe.

We reached the backside of a large tent. I motioned for Josiah, Valentina, and Nadie to remain there with Elan for protection. They gathered together, held hands, and closed their eyes.

While they worked at seeing what brought the daemons here and what their future plans might be, Samson and I snuck inside the tent. If something went wrong, Elan and I could connect. We weren't far apart, just the fabric of the shelter between us.

Inside, we found a bedding area—what looked like a pile of furs and blankets heaped together. A table sat in the middle, with maps and other writing I didn't recognize scattered over the top. A single torch lit the space.

Before we moved any further, I asked Elan if he could see our shadows from outside. When he replied that he couldn't, I moved to the table.

Any idea what this is? Samson asked privately.

No idea. Taking out my not-quite-useless cell phone, I snapped pictures of everything. I took a last look around, feeling as if we were missing something.

Wait. I think if I.... Samson stepped to the table and picked up one of the parchments. He studied it, his fingers brushing over the unusual letters. I realized then what he was trying to do—use his gift on the written word.

Before I could ask if it worked, someone spoke. "We have to hurry, Kayne. We don't have much time."

The voice came just past the front flap. I pushed Samson back toward the ground so he could slip out. Without question, he dropped and rolled. Another voice—presumably Kayne—spoke. "You think I don't know that, Irvyn? Now shut up and help me."

They entered, found me on my hands and one knee about to duck under the flap. I looked up, met the dark gaze of the first daemon to enter. He stared back, shock and censure running across his face. The second daemon nearly slammed into him he'd stopped so fast. "Kayne, what are you—"

Irvyn stopped, stared. I could sense Samson's panic, his voice screaming in my mind to get out, to run. Yet I couldn't move. I felt trapped by Kayne's glittering gaze.

More daemons moved about outside the tent. We all could hear them, plain as if they were in the same room. A strange buzzing sound assaulted my brain, and I winced in pain. Then a voice broke through and spoke into my mind. It shocked me, for I knew it was the daemon's voice. But the connection was different than when I spoke to Samson, and even different still from telepathy with animals.

He spoke, but I didn't think I could respond in kind. He said one word. Urgently. *Go.*

I dropped, rolled. Samson caught me and hauled me to my feet. And as one, we moved out. We made it over the hill before I heard from Lenna. *Lani, we're under attack.*

She kept her voice calm, yet her fear beat at me. Scooping up Elan in his wolf form—a surprised yip huffing from his lungs—I put on a burst of speed and sent a call to Frances. *We need you and the shifters.* Sending him the coordinates we were headed to, I next spoke to Samson. *Group one is under attack. Get the others to safety.*

I'm coming with you.

Please, Samson. Josiah, Valentina, and Nadie need you. Get them to safety first, then come to me.

He growled and spit a few choice words in response, but I knew he'd do as I asked. With some skill and a whole lot of luck, by the time Samson arrived, we wouldn't need his help. As I moved, I called out to the contact in group three, though I worried they were too far from the fight to get there in time.

Using my preternatural speed—even with the added burden of Elan—I found group one in seconds. Smoothly setting Elan on his feet, I continued forward to meet the threat head-on. Lenna whirled to charge with me, her brother at her side. The rest of the group halted in their tracks and turned to face the enemy.

Fifteen daemons charged after us, lips snarling and fists raised. For a split second, I met the leader's gaze and felt his hesitation. His strange, golden eyes spit fire at me, and I met him with my own fist, making contact low in his gut and slipping under his guard. Lenna took him on as I aimed a kick at the next daemon's knee. It slowed him down long enough for Elan to sink his teeth into his chest.

I didn't stop, couldn't stop. Moving smooth as water, graceful as a gazelle, lethal as a lion, I spun and dipped and struck my opponents with deadly accuracy. They fought back, but it didn't seem as if they aimed to kill. Whatever they were here for, it wasn't to fight.

It was to capture. The earth trembled around me; fire rained down. It struck the daemons with a pop and hiss of melting skin. From behind me, I heard a heart-wrenching howl of pain. For a moment, I turned and saw Elan hit the ground hard, his ribs jutting out at unnatural angles. With a roar of pure rage, Lenna lunged toward him, attacking as she burst through a wall of daemons to stand protectively over her brother.

In that split second that I became distracted, a daemon grabbed my wrist and wrapped an arm around my throat. He dragged me back, his hot breath on my neck. Before I could do anything to release myself, a gush of wind flew over my head and smacked him straight in the forehead.

His arm slackened as he grunted in pain. Frances appeared in the middle of the maelstrom, the shifter brothers not far behind.

"Help Lenna!" I shouted at him as I spun and added the force of wind in my own attack.

Lenna had been surrounded, her teeth barely keeping her attackers at bay. Elan groaned in pain on the ground, and I knew we didn't have much time to get him to a healer. We had to end this now.

Frances threw out spell after spell, working his way toward Lenna. I did my best to reach her while Atienn and Chayton fought their own battle. We were hurting the daemons; they were now out for blood. One got past Lenna's guard and went to wrap his muscular arms around her body with crushing intent. Before he could complete the action, another daemon stepped in, gripped the attacker by his shoulders, and tossed him aside. Frances and I stared in shock even as we pushed forward.

The daemon who had saved Lenna from attack looked down at her as if a battle weren't raging around them. He reached out as if to stroke along her muzzle, but she snapped her sharp teeth, and he thought better of it.

Group three arrived en force, surrounding the daemons and shouting battle cries.

"Retreat," the same daemon called out, his eyes never leaving Lenna's. I couldn't understand what was happening. He seemed protective of the wolf-girl for reasons I couldn't fathom. When the daemons didn't stop, he shouted, "I said, retreat!"

One by one, they backed off. The daemon with the golden eyes—his palm pressing against a gaping wound on his ribs—snarled at us and his own men. The one who had called retreat finally looked away from Lenna and loaned his shoulder to the golden-eyed leader. Atienn and Chayton stood back-to-back, panting heavily and watching our attackers warily. Frances kept his guard up as I lurched forward and finally reached Lenna and the injured Elan. Lenna kept up a low growl, baring her teeth to get her point across.

The earth split open with a great crack, sucking the daemons beneath the surface. It closed with an ear-splitting bang, and we all stared, stunned.

Some of group one, who had been assisting the fight with their manipulation powers, sank to the ground with sheer exhaustion. They'd pushed themselves beyond anything they'd ever tried before. I was so proud of them.

Of all of them.

"Frances, we need to get Elan to the healers. Is anyone else injured?"

"Cuts and scrapes, some weak. Nothing serious," one of the still-standing element manipulators told me.

Headlights bounced over the tough terrain, and I looked up to see a jeep racing to us. Before it came to a stop, Samson jumped out, ran to me, and wrapped his arms around my back. "You're okay, you're okay, you're okay."

"Of course," I assured him, giving myself a moment to soak up his warmth. "Elan needs help."

"Good thing I brought some."

His mom pushed out of the jeep, along with one of the doctors from the reservation. Everyone moved back except Lenna, who hovered over her brother. Neveah said, "We need him to shift back. I'm not a veterinarian."

Elan's tongue wagged out, laughing even through his pain. I knelt by his side and placed a hand against his head. "Frances will clothe you as you shift, Elan. It's going to hurt, but we need you to do this." To Lenna, I added, *I can clothe you if you'd like to shift. Your brother needs you.*

She didn't wait. Her form shimmered, flew apart, and slammed together again. She now crouched on the ground, the plain clothes giving her a semblance of modesty. I stood so she could take my place at his head, murmuring encouragement for him to shift through the pain.

I asked everyone else to back away to give Neveah and the doctor space to work. Frances and I checked over the rest of group one, distributing water that Samson had thought to bring.

Though he tried to tough it out, Elan's hoarse shouts of pain filled the night air. We all winced, knowing it was a necessary evil. More headlights cut across the night, driving at a more sedate pace than Samson had been. "Oh good, the rescue crew is here."

"Good thinking," I said. "Let's get everyone loaded up and back to the community center."

While group three helped group one climb into vehicles, Frances, Samson, and I waited to protect Elan, Lenna, and the healers until Elan could be transported. Frances and Samson loaded him into the jeep as soon as they were able, Lenna crouched in the little bit of space on the floor of the backseat to keep him from being jostled around. The doctor and Neveah took up the front and headed back to town.

Frances looked me over. "You need blood."

"So do you. You've put a lot into taking down the barrier. Any progress?"

"Nothing to talk about. Domingo and the others are still there; Chayton and Atienn went back to protect them. Let's go home, see to our needs. Then we can meet everyone back at the center and figure out what the hell just happened."

I looked at Samson and held my hand out. "Feel like flying?"

Chapter 11

As we flew through the red haze, I could feel my body beginning to sag. Adrenaline had sustained me, but now that the fighting was done, I needed to rest and replenish.

"Drink from me," Samson murmured against my ear.

Startled, I looked at him and shook my head. "I can't."

"Why?"

"The pull between mates...it's strong. It wouldn't just be replenishing, it would be...arousing."

His eyes widened, and I could feel his skin heat at my words. I swallowed hard, fighting my opposing feelings on claiming my mate versus keeping him safe. It would happen sooner rather than later.

But not now. Not in the middle of a war.

"Thank you," I said quietly as we began our descent. "Your offer means a lot to me."

"I would do anything for you."

We landed, our arms still wrapped around the other. I looked up at his dark gaze, filled with love and longing. Same as mine. "I love you, Samson."

He stilled, his heart skipping a beat before thudding hard. "Really?"

"Yes. You blindsided me, and I didn't want what's between us, but I know I can't live without it or you. Your courage terrifies me, and your carefree, giving nature baffles me. You are like my own personal sun. I didn't know what was missing without you, the darkness that had all but consumed me. Now, I would wither and die if you weren't in my life. I know I'll spend many years proving I can be your mate, but I'm ready and willing to do whatever it takes. I love you."

He didn't respond with words. His mouth captured mine, at first soft and sweet. It turned hungry, needy. My heart stuttered, nearly burst with happiness. With the love I felt for the man in my arms.

My mate.

"Stop making out, guys. We have daemons to beat."

Samson pulled back with a grin, his eyes sparkling with love and lust and happiness. "We'll pick this up later."

"Later," I agreed, slightly stunned.

We turned with hands clasped. Frances leaned casually against the door frame, bags of blood in his hands. He tossed one to me before ripping open his own.

"This won't disgust you, will it?"

"I don't think so," Samson replied.

"Okay. Just don't look at me."

"A nearly impossible task."

"You two are making me gag on my dinner here," Frances said with a groan. "Seriously, if I'd known you'd be this cutesy, I wouldn't have encouraged this relationship."

"Shut up, Frances," Samson and I said simultaneously. We grinned at each other as I ripped open the bag of blood and drank from it. Samson didn't stare, but he didn't cringe away, either.

Making quick work of the task, I felt an instant rejuvenation. The blood flowed through my veins, replenishing depleted cells and giving me a boost of energy. "You need to eat, Samson. As do the rest."

"I'll grab a sandwich when we get back. I did want to tell you about what Josiah, Valentina, and Nadie told me."

"Anything helpful?"

"Valentina and Nadie, not really. They both have hidden their gift all their lives, so even admitting to having them was difficult. Valentina said she got a small flash of daemons gathered together in the same area we were in. She said it looked as if they were performing a ritual. The moon was full, but other than that, she had no details."

"That could be anytime in the next two nights."

"Nadie got nothing. She said she usually sees possible futures through touch—she tried by placing her hands on the earth, but it didn't work. I didn't think you'd want her that close to any of the daemons."

"Definitely not," I said, my mouth tipping up at one corner. "And Josiah?"

"His gift is different. He can see any event in a certain place throughout time. The best way to describe it is fast-forwarding a VHS tape to find the spot you want. It takes time. He was able to pinpoint the day and time the daemons arrived—it coincides with our second trip to the cave. They just sort of...appeared."

"All right. If anything, it confirmed our suspicions. Before we go to the center, I also wanted to talk about this," I said, pulling out my phone and scrolling through the pictures. "Did your gift work on the pages?"

"It did. I've never tried to use it on the written word before, so it took longer than I'd have liked. I can translate while you tell us what the hell happened in that tent."

Handing the phone over, I relayed my experience after pushing Samson to safety. "The daemons are obviously not on our side, but it seems they might have a few rebels. We may not be able to trust them, but it seemed as if Kayne and Irvyn, at the very least, didn't wish me harm. The same with the one on the battlefield—he protected Lenna when she would have been crushed. We need to find out more."

"Some of these are spells, from what I can tell. A lot of darkness."

"That tracks with what Valentina saw. What else?"

"Maps of this area but also of towns in other countries. I have a feeling we're not their only stop."

Frances looked disturbed. "What other countries?"

"Romania, Ireland, and Australia, to name a few."

Frances looked at me, took a deep breath, and let it out again. "Samson, I think it's time I tell you more about me. I'd prefer if this stayed between us, at least for now."

Frances had Samson's full attention. "Of course, man."

"Like Lani, I am an Elemental. But for a long time, I was something else—something darker. Our people call them shadowmen." Hands in his pockets, Frances straightened his spine and met Samson's gaze head-on. "My parents were murdered in front of me, my sister was lost to me. I turned to the darkness very young. It is a constant pull for our kind, especially without our mate to anchor us. Mine hit me sooner because of my family. Others last hundreds of years without turning or even being tempted.

"When my family was taken away from me, I took the small part of me that was left—the light, the happiness—and locked it away. I allowed the darkness to fester, to take over. When I found other Elementals, I converted them to my side, brought them over to the darkness.

"I'm not proud of what I've done. If I could go back...but I cannot. I can only move forward. Thanks to Jade, I have been given a second chance. She found that locked up part of me, brought it out. Risked herself to do so. I owe my life to her."

Samson reached out, clapped a hand on his upper arm. "We all have a choice, every day, to be better than we were the day before. You've taken that step. I see it, Lani sees it. I trust you, Frances."

Emotions swamped Frances, but he manfully pushed them aside. "I tell you that so you understand where I come from, what I've seen. There were rumors of an alliance between other shadowmen and creatures more powerful than ourselves. I brushed these rumors off—the darkness made me believe no one or no thing could be more powerful than me—but now, seeing these daemons for myself, I believe them to be true."

"You think the daemons and the shadowmen are working together?"

"More than that. I think the daemons are turning Elementals into shadowmen."

Sucking in a shocked breath, I straightened, thinking through the implications. "This reservation. Romania. Ireland. Australia. What do they have in common?"

"Their folklore," Samson said.

"Exactly. This reservation is swarming with Gifted. I bet the same is true in those other countries. And during the fight, at least at first, they weren't aiming to kill. What if—what if they're here to recruit?"

"We need to get back to the community center."

When we arrived, we found several guards watching from the shadows. Samson held his hands out in a gesture of peace, though I was certain our lack of horns alone showed that we were not the enemy.

Striding through the doors, I first went into the room set up as an infirmary. I wanted to see how Elan fared and to speak with Lenna. Frances came with me while Samson went to speak with his family.

Elan lay on a cot, shirtless but with gauze wrapped around his waist and chest. He grinned on seeing me, though I could see the edge of pain behind his dark eyes. "How are you feeling?"

"I'm fine. It was just a scratch."

Lenna rolled her eyes from her position on the ground. "You weren't in a sword fight, moron. You were nearly crushed to death."

"Yeah, but I've always wanted to say that."

Frances stepped forward, introduced himself since he'd been at the border when our groups formed, and there wasn't much time for chitchat when he'd joined the battle. "I can speed up your healing if you'd permit me."

Elan looked doubtful. "What do I have to do?"

Leaving the men to discuss that, I asked Lenna to speak privately. We walked to a corner of the room—it was as private as we could manage at the moment. "How are you holding up?"

"Better, now that I know Elan will be okay."

"You two are close. Twins, right?"

"That's right."

"Do you have telepathy with him?"

She nodded. "We've never told anyone, not even our parents."

"It's all right. Telepathy between twins is normal for my people. I have a feeling other twins here can do the same, whether or not they've tried." I paused and studied the young woman for a moment. Her red-rimmed eyes and the bruised smudges just below gave away her weariness, but I also saw a strength in her gaze that told me she could handle my questions. "You protected your brother like a warrior. But that daemon almost had you—should have had you. Believe me, I'm thankful that he didn't, but the other daemon saved your life."

She looked down now, fear sneaking into her eyes. "I know he did."

"Did he speak to you?"

"N-no. Just when he said retreat, but he wasn't speaking to me."

"Lenna," I said gently. "Did he speak to you telepathically?"

Tears glimmered in her eyes. Not just fear but stark terror washed over her face. "Yes."

Going on instinct, I wrapped my arms around her. She sagged against me and let a few tears escape. "It's going to be all right. Can you tell me what he said?"

"He said a word I didn't recognize. Grādh."

Do you recognize the word grādh? I asked privately to Samson.

After a moment, he replied, *It's old Irish Gaelic for love or beloved.*

Having a human translator sure came in handy. *The daemon who saved Lenna called her that telepathically.*

What does that mean?

I hesitated before answering. *I think it means our situation just got a whole lot more complicated.* Pulling back from Lenna, I held her upper arms and met her watery gaze. "Did you speak back to him?"

"No," she said, shaking her head to add emphasis. "Should I have?"

"Not if you don't want to. Has he spoken to you since?"

"No, but I—I can feel him there. Do you know what I mean?"

"I do." The same way I could feel Samson. "Lenna, I don't think he means you any harm. He saved your life, got the others to back off. But we know nothing about them."

"I'm scared," she admitted in a low voice.

"You're allowed to be. We're going to find a way through this. I promise." Glancing over, I saw Frances had finished giving Elan blood. A small infusion of his Elemental blood would speed up Elan's recovery without affecting him long-term. I motioned him over, then said to Lenna, "Why don't you go back with your brother? He should be able to rest easier now."

She nodded and began to walk away. Stopping, she looked back and said, "Thank you."

I watched as she made her way back to Elan's side, as Frances walked to mine. "What was that about?" he asked.

"Let's go find Samson. I'll fill you in on the way."

Chapter 12

Samson met Frances and me outside of the community center, and I filled them both in on my theory about Lenna and the daemon that had saved her. "You think the daemons could have mates?"

Looking at Frances, I shrugged. "Do you have a better explanation?"

"No, but—that seems crazy."

"Any crazier than what we are?" I had him there, and he knew it. "We need to speak with the group as a whole. Did Viktor and Santiago fill everyone in while we were gone?"

"They did. My dad used his special ability to keep everyone calm," Samson said. "Why don't we gather all the kids in a room together while we hold a council of sorts?"

"That's a great idea. We can put a few of the older kids in charge—like Kai."

"I'll get some of my family to help. Give us a few minutes."

"I'd like to go back to the border, but I'd also like to be part of this meeting," Frances said once Samson walked away.

"I'd like you here, too. Hold on," I said, then held up a hand as I contacted Atienn. *How is everyone holding up? Frances is going to be here for a little while. Do any of you need to come back?*

Everyone's fine. Our dad is under strict orders not to exhaust himself.

No sign of daemons?

None.

If there is, run. Get the others to safety. Do your best not to engage, but reach out to me immediately. Understand?

You got it.

"They're fine at the border, for now. You can relieve them after this meeting."

Samson, Raven, their parents, and extended family quietly moved about the room, shuffling the children to the next. I saw Kai argue but eventually relent, taking Koko and Kaiah's hands as they moved. She was the oldest of that group but still so young.

Children should be allowed to be children for as long as possible. But when war comes to their doorstep, there is only so much shielding a parent can do.

Once the kids were safely tucked away, Viktor grabbed everyone's attention and started us off. "Thank you all for your cooperation. We are strongest together, and I know everyone will do their part in eradicating this new threat."

He nodded at me, so I took over the floor. "Hello, everyone that I haven't met yet. I'm Lani, and I believe Viktor and Santiago have explained the situation and what I am. We took recon groups out to the daemon settlement and were attacked on our way back. Elan suffered the worst of the injuries, but he is healing as we speak.

"Samson and I found maps in the settlement, not only of the reservation but of various towns around the world. We believe the daemons are looking for new Gifted to recruit to the darkness."

A wave of murmurs spread across the room. Once they settled, I continued. "There seemed to be a few of the daemons who did not mean us harm. Two found me in the settlement but did not attack. Instead, they made sure I left before others spotted me. Another saved Lenna's life and issued the order to retreat. This is new territory for me, and I'd like to ask all of you now if any of your stories tell us more about these creatures."

A weathered elder, his once strong limbs now shaking with age, rose to speak. Despite his physical fragility, he exuded a quiet authority that commanded the attention of those around him. As he began to speak, his voice carried a weight of experience and held a quiet authority. "Any stories involving the defeat of the twins are spotty, at best. Daemons are mentioned briefly, but there are a few facts that seem consistent. Their physical appearance seems to be accurate. They are strongest in the three nights of the full moon. It was said they could not control their nature during this time, but otherwise, they were able to blend into human society if they so wished."

"They would still stand out, with their size," Frances said.

"True," the elder replied. "As I've said, accounts are spotty."

"It makes sense, though. We are also most powerful in the full moon." My eyebrows furrowed as I thought this through. Perhaps it wasn't my fault that the daemons arrived now. My vision in the Divining Pool could have simply been a warning of their arrival, not the cause. "Is there anything else?"

A woman stood this time and cleared her throat. "When I was a girl, my great-grandmother told me stories that her own grandmother had told her. Daemons were used as the boogeyman to warn children not to wander alone in the night. She believed, but I never took much stock in the stories. I should have."

"How could you know?" I asked rhetorically. "What do you remember of the stories?"

"Bits and pieces, only. Mostly warnings. One that stuck out to me was of a girl, just into womanhood, who wandered the desert at night and came across an injured creature such as these. It put her under its spell, and every night, she would go to it, care for it. She would come home each morning with marks on her neck, her wrists. And then, one morning, she never came home."

I glanced first to Frances, then to Samson, sure the same thought went through their heads as my own. "Thank you. Is there anyone else that remembers any stories?"

A few spoke up, but nothing new came to light. We still had very little to go on—enough to make assumptions only. Frances leaned close. "We need to set up guards and make sure everyone gets some sleep. I'll take over at the border."

"You need someone with you. I'll come with."

"Get everything organized here first. I'll go out, escort Domingo and the others back so they can rest. You can go with me then."

Giving him a nod, I turned back to the group. "We'd like to set up security around the center in four-hour shifts. Everyone needs to try to get some rest while we figure out the next steps."

"We should attack while they're vulnerable," one of the men spoke up. "During the day."

Several nodded or shouted their agreement. "I agree. But let's get some rest first, all right? We'll meet together again before dawn."

Leaving them to talk amongst themselves, I went back to the infirmary, Samson at my side. "I want to come with you when you go to the wall."

"You need to rest, Samson."

"I need to be with you."

Facing him, I took his hands in mine. "Please. You need your strength for tomorrow, as I'm certain I won't be able to talk you out of joining the attack. We can communicate at any time. I promise to contact you if anything goes wrong. You can reach out anytime you need, even if you don't speak. We can feel each other at all times."

"I hate this."

"As do I, but we both know it's necessary."

His hands cupped my cheeks and pulled me to him. His lips crushed down on mine, a promise of things to come. "I love you."

"I love you, too. I want to check on Elan before I go. Fill them in on what we have planned."

Samson walked with me. When we entered the doorway, I spotted little Koko wandering through the maze of cots, placing a palm on a patient's arm, sometimes just briefly, sometimes saying a few words. Niko had told us she was an empath; I imagined she felt the need to help those she could.

"She's so young," I murmured. "But look at her power. Watch her, make sure she doesn't take on too much."

"I will," Samson promised.

I went over to Elan; Lenna still sat on the ground, her head resting against the cot as she dozed. Kneeling beside her, I nudged her gently. "You should find a cot."

"I'm fine," she mumbled. "Everything okay?"

Elan's eyes popped open, so I filled them both in on the plan. "You won't join us unless you're cleared by the doctor."

He frowned, but Lenna said, "I will. I can fight."

Nodding, I squeezed her arm in reassurance. "I'd be proud to fight at your side. Get some rest now, proper rest. You'll need it."

Frances brought Domingo and the other two helpers back, Atienn and Chayton in their wake. The shifter boys looked exhausted, so I put them under orders to eat and rest. Frances studied Samson for a moment as we were getting ready to leave, and he pulled me aside. "You should stay with Samson."

"Why?"

"Lani, you two need a little time to yourselves. Take it. We don't know what tomorrow will bring."

"But—"

"But nothing; I can take care of myself. If anything happens, I'll shift and call out to you. Trust me, take tonight to be with your mate."

I looked over to Samson, saw the weariness in his eyes. But more than that, a deep-seated fear. "All right, but you don't hesitate to reach me."

"Promise."

As he left, I walked over to Samson. He'd watched Frances leave and had the question all over his face. "Frances convinced me to stay. Would you—would you go somewhere with me?"

All tension and strain cleared from his gaze. "Anywhere."

"Let's talk to your dad and uncle first." We found them in the main room, making sure everyone settled for the night. After I explained that we were leaving for a little while, I said, "Any shifter, in their animal form, can call me back at any time. Anything comes up, don't hesitate. You all get some rest. Samson and I will be back before dawn."

We left together, hand in hand. When we got outside, I nodded in greeting to the guards, then wrapped my arms around Samson and blurred us from sight. We rose into the air together, but he never looked away from my face. Traveling under the strange red haze, I brought us to the house we'd rented, placing our feet on the doorstep.

"Frances said we should have some time together."

"Remind me to thank him later."

Before I could respond, his mouth captured mine. We managed to push inside the door and stumble into the living room. I lit all the candles with a thought, both there and in my bedroom. I couldn't give him much at the moment, but I could give him candlelight.

My back hit a wall, but I didn't mind. My hands went to the hem of his shirt and yanked it over his head. As my palms smoothed down his chest, I heard his intake of breath. He returned the favor, his dark gaze glittering with desire as he cupped me, tasted my skin. His arms wrapped around my waist and lifted. I complied by securing my legs around his hips.

He moved us down the hall and into the bedroom. Candles were scattered along any available surface. Their soft scents filled the room, their flickering light reflected in Samson's gaze when he pulled back to look at me.

"You are so beautiful," he murmured. "I don't know how I got so lucky."

"You kept badgering me until I said yes," I reminded him with a grin. Then my expression turned serious, softened. "But I am the lucky one. I don't deserve you."

"What did I say before?" he asked gently. "Silly, beautiful woman. You are everything to me. My literal dream girl come to life. You have done more good in the world than I could ever hope to. If anyone is undeserving, it's me."

"Why don't we just call it a tie?"

"Sounds good to me." And to seal the deal, he pressed his lips back to mine.

We fell to the bed, our legs entwined. We explored each other with our hands, our tongues. Fire sizzled through my veins as his fingers teased along my skin. I arched into him when his mouth closed over my breast.

I needed him like air to breathe. Couldn't wait another second to be one. This was my first time, as it was his. Yet somehow, we moved and touched and tasted as if we'd done this for millennia. He built me up, held me on the edge. The release came with a shuddering of breath, a tremble of limbs. New sensations washed over and through me, yet all I wanted was more.

I asked, and Samson delivered. Before I knew it, I teetered on the ledge again. "Please, Samson."

"I want to make sure you're ready."

"I am. I want you. Join us together. Make us one."

He couldn't resist the plea of his mate. He slid inside, and I came apart even through the bite of pain. Shaking, panting, I had no words for the way it felt to finally, finally be with Samson. He gripped my hands and looked deep into my eyes. "Are you all right?"

"Yes," I managed to say through gasps. To prove it, I kissed him passionately. One leg wrapped around his back, and I arched into him, encouraging him to move.

He took it slow and easy, even when I asked for more. My muscles wound tighter and tighter, the build like smoldering embers suddenly erupting into flame. Only when I cried out did he begin to move with abandon. His own hoarse cry rose to the heavens, made all the candles grow and flicker.

Shuddering, shaking, we lay in each other's arms as our hearts slowed to a steady pace. I'd never felt so fulfilled, so content. Even in the midst of a war, Samson was my safe haven.

Suddenly, I had something to live for. Something to die for. Our lives had just begun, and I would do anything to protect our future. I would do anything to protect my mate.

Chapter 13

Samson and I arrived back at the community center just before dawn. We hadn't slept much, yet I had a strange, wonderful kind of energy flowing through me. When we'd finally forced ourselves to rise and dress, I'd also made sure Samson ate breakfast while I filled up on blood.

We would both need our strength for the coming battle.

There was plenty of activity already; while most had managed to grab a few hours of sleep, others rounded up weapons of all kinds. Paco and Kitchi were in charge of sorting, with the help of Josiah and Lenna. The young woman seemed to have a will of steel. She would need it for what was to come.

"I'd like to send out a scouting party," I said once Viktor and Santiago joined us in the weapons room. "We need to find out what they're up to and where."

"Who do you suggest?" Viktor asked.

"Any shifters willing. We need to be quick and silent and be able to communicate. I'll lead it."

"I'm in," Lenna said. "Elan would rather rest and be ready to fight."

"Count me in, too," a new voice said. I turned and got introduced to Lenna's mom, Celia. "As is my brother."

"You're both shifters, as well." I remembered them from the night before, though I hadn't known their relation to Elan and Lenna. They'd volunteered to protect the community center.

She straightened her back proudly. "Damn right, we are. Where do you think my children inherited such a gift?"

Lenna grinned and wrapped an arm around Celia's waist. I couldn't help but like these two firecrackers. "Happy to have you. Where is your brother?"

"Roger Salvatore," he said on entering the room. "Nice to meet you."

Tayen's dad, Samson supplied.

"Nice to meet you, as well. I think four is plenty for recon. We can come in from each direction. I'm guessing you two can speak telepathically?" Roger and Celia nodded. "And you all can speak to me once you're in your animal form. Lean and fast."

"Agreed. When should we leave?"

"The sooner the better. I'm not sure if the daemons will be around during the day, so I'd like to catch them before the sun fully rises. Are you three ready now?"

"Let's do this," Celia said.

I turned to Samson and squeezed his hand. "I'll be back soon."

Though I could see that he wanted to argue, I appreciated that he didn't. He also didn't try to convince me he should go with. He trusted me to do this and come back to him. "I love you. Be safe."

"I love you, too." Kissing him on the cheek, I turned and gestured for the three shifters to follow me. We went into the night, and I allowed them to shift in privacy.

It was different than an Elemental shifting. We were able to transform into the air itself before choosing our animal form. With the Gifted, they all seemed to have only one form—the wolf. To make it easier, they stripped down first and then allowed the animal to take over.

Though, now that I thought about it, I wondered if they were able to shift into others—or at least the eagle. According to their cave paintings, the original twins could do either. It was something to talk about later.

Once they were shifted, I spoke into each of their minds. Lenna was already used to it from our exploits the day before, but this would be the first time Celia and Roger had spoken to anyone but each other.

Celia, take the north. Roger, take the east. Lenna, west. I'll wrap around and come in from the south. I sent the words into their minds simultaneously—something else Frances had me work on before this madness. When they responded, only I heard it, but it helped cut down on time. *If you see anything, don't hesitate to reach out.*

We ran in silence, splitting off to go our own ways. Using my supernatural speed, I managed to circle around, nearly hitting the southern barrier before moving in toward the camp. I could see a flurry of activity, so I found a high perch to stop and watch.

I still couldn't hear anything, but it seemed they were preparing to leave the area for the day. Maybe they went underground while the sun was high. Our records on daemons were too inconsistent to know for sure.

There was movement a couple hundred feet to my right. Shifting into the form of a sparrow and settling in a pine bough, I waited and watched. A huge, hulking, dark form came into view and paused not twenty feet away.

I recognized Kayne from the campground. He stood, staring down at the encampment, his dark gaze troubled.

I mean you no harm. I would just like to talk. His words floated across my mind, startling me. Of course he knew I was there.

I took wing and landed on my two feet. Neither of us moved closer. We both watched the activity below with passive interest. "What would you like to talk about?"

"You plan on attacking today. You should wait until tonight."

I didn't question how he knew of our plan. "When you're stronger?"

"When they're distracted."

I looked over at him now, studied his profile. He could be handsome if he ever smiled—though the horns gave me pause. "When will they be distracted?"

"At midnight, they will perform a full moon ritual. It is the first step in creating shadowmen from your Gifted—and it is the best time to get the upper hand."

"Why are you helping us?"

He finally met my gaze. His eyes weren't as dark as I'd originally thought; they were a deep, deep green. And as the first rays of light broke over the horizon, I noticed golden streaks in the otherwise brown hair. "Just because I'm a daemon doesn't make me a devil."

"There are others like you, aren't there?"

"Yes."

"Will you stand with us when the time comes?"

"It is not so simple." He looked back, his jaw ticking with tension.

"Explain it to me, please. My mate is here. This is his family, their land. What do they want?"

"What all true daemons want. Their souls."

The answer left a pit of dread in my gut. "Are you not a true daemon?"

"We don't have time for chitchat. If you want to survive, your best bet is midnight tonight. Whatever you do, don't let that ritual take place."

Before I could ask another question, he was gone.

One by one, the daemons in the camp slipped into the earth. We had no way to attack them now, even if we wanted to. Letting out a breath, I reached out to the others in my recon. *Meet me back at the center. We need to talk.*

We gathered once again, and I relayed my conversation with Kayne.

"We can't trust him."

That seemed to be the recurring theme. The same sentiment, expressed in a myriad of ways, had been tossed out for the last twenty minutes. And while I appreciated their input, it was time to put my foot down. "When we infiltrated their camp yesterday, Kayne let me go. Now, he's given us valuable information. They disappear underground during the day—I'm not sure if they're sensitive to the sun or if they're using the time to plan, but I believe him."

"Either way, there's nothing we can do now," Roger finally said. "We all saw them disappear. Valentina saw them gathered together under the full moon—that's enough corroboration for me."

Sending him a grateful smile, I turned back to Viktor. Ultimately, it was his decision, his people he was putting on the line. With a heavy sigh, he nodded. "We attack at midnight."

His proclamation immediately launched us all into gear. I sent Chayton and Atienn to retrieve Frances from the border, where he still worked at unraveling the barrier. We needed his help here.

After explaining to the bulk of the group what was going on, we asked for volunteers to fight. After the last couple of days, I wasn't surprised when the majority stepped forward. The core group of us—along with any that possessed military experience—planned strategy, then split the volunteers into groups accordingly.

I worked with the fighters on targeting the daemons' weaknesses, while Frances helped the Gifted unveil their true abilities. Judging by what Frances and that group were able to accomplish in just a few short hours, I couldn't wait to see what they could do when they had years of practice.

Viktor, Santiago, and the other military veterans worked with the non-Gifted using the weapons they'd managed to scrounge from homes. At the end of the day, everyone looked exhausted but battle-ready.

Viktor ordered them all to get some rest. We'd move out at eleven o'clock.

I found Samson and a dark corner where we could hold on to each other. A nervous energy hummed in the air, and I could see worry on even the youngest of faces. They gave me the courage to do whatever it would take to keep Samson and his family safe. This whole reservation had also become my family over the short time I'd been here.

"You should try to sleep," I said.

"I'm not sure I can."

"Come here." Guiding him to lie down so his head pillowed on my lap, I stroked my fingers through his hair and gazed down into his dark eyes. "I'll watch over you."

"I know," he said, reaching up to stroke my cheek. "Lani, there's something I want to talk to you about."

"All right."

"When this is over, and we've won, I want to become like you."

My heartbeat turned into a thud. "You want to be converted?"

"Yes. I love you, and I want to be with you. You love me, and you want to be with me. So, why not?"

"It's not so easy a decision."

"It is if it means being with you."

I searched his gaze for a long time. His love shone bright, beating at me through our connection. How could I say no to him? "Okay. When this is over, when we've won, we'll figure out the best way to convert you."

He sat up so that our mouths were even and drew me into a kiss. In a room surrounded by his extended family, we had to be careful not to get carried away. When I pulled gently away, he sighed happily and rested his head against my thighs.

"Sleep now," I murmured, running my fingers through his thick hair again. "We have a big night ahead of us."

∞ ∞ ∞

ALL CREWS GATHERED OUTSIDE AT ten-thirty. I was in the lead crew, along with Samson, Frances, and most of the shifters. Our plan was to surround the settlement and hit them from every direction at once. My group had the furthest to go; like earlier, we'd be circling around to head in from the south.

Nerves and trepidation hung thick in the air as families bid tearful goodbyes. I hated seeing this. Samson squeezed my hand, and I knew we were on the same page. We would do whatever it took to bring them all back.

Frances cast a spell over each group to cloak them from view. We needed every little bit of help we could take. When we gave the signal to head out, Frances and I boosted our group's movements to remain quick and silent since we had the furthest to go. The desert itself seemed unnaturally silent; even the animals trapped under this strange barrier seemed to know something was about to go down.

We followed much the same path as I had that morning. When we came upon the hilltop where I'd spoken with Kayne, I gave the signal to pause and wait. Below, the daemons had already begun to gather around a wide bonfire, the tips of the flames easily reaching over even the tallest of the creature's heads.

I could see Kayne standing with Irvyn, their arms crossed as they surveyed the scene. The one who had saved Lenna stood not far from them, stoic in his resolve to participate.

The obvious leader—the man with strange, golden eyes that stood closer to seven and a half feet tall—directed the others in preparation for the spell. A strange sense of familiarity passed over me, but I put it down to nerves. At my count, there were at least thirty daemons now. While we outnumbered them, I didn't know if our skills would hold up.

Except they had to. We had no other choice. The fact that the daemons wanted to convert the tribe instead of killing them also weighed heavily in our favor.

The other teams contacted me within minutes of each other, signaling that they were in position. All the daemons stepped closer to the fire as the leader held his hands out, his head tipped back as he chanted. One of them threw herbs or a powder into the flames, making them billow even higher into the sky.

It was time. I gave the signal and spoke simultaneously to the shifters in each group. We charged.

Our silent attack worked until we bumped into whatever magical barrier the daemons had erected around their camp. As soon as we crossed over, the leader's eyes popped open, and he glared at our intrusion. The rest of the daemons spun and put their guards up, their spears too far away to be useful. Some released knives from their belts, while others created balls of magic fire with their hands.

The need for stealth was done. I let loose a bolstering battle cry and aimed for my first target. The clash was nearly deafening as wolves snapped and bit and howled. Fists met flesh, weapons fired and clashed. Most of the daemons relied on brute strength, but those that conjured spells were met with the likes of Frances.

Colliding magic rained sparks down as fights broke out all around the camp. The daemons were outnumbered, but they were strong and ridiculously fast. As I ducked an attack and issued my own, my eyes met Kayne's. He defended his camp, but I noticed he didn't deliver any maiming blows. He redirected attacks and managed to keep his aggressor from harm. It looked effortless on his part, which concerned me.

It also became painfully obvious that while he might want us to succeed, he wouldn't do anything about it outright.

There was nothing I could do about it now. I moved like a shadow, assisting members of the tribe when I saw them stumble. Some daemons were able to retrieve their spears; Samson clashed with one, got overpowered. Before the daemon could strike, I slipped a clawed hand through his back and into a kidney.

He dropped with a roar of pain. Gripping Samson's forearm, I hauled him to his feet, and we went back-to-back. More came at us. I went on the offensive, lunging and spinning and evading the daemon's lethal strikes. One charged with his spear. I ducked and went to the side and brought up my knee to his sternum. He grunted with pain and tried to bring the spear around to whack me in the head.

With one arm, I blocked his swing, and with my free hand, I gripped the spear. When he tried to pull away, I slammed my arm against his elbow.

The daemon released the spear with a cry of pain, and I spun to face the next threat.

A pair of golden eyes met mine over the span of several feet. His lips pulled back in a snarl, and I brought the newly acquired spear around to defend. Perhaps if I could take the leader out, the rest would give up.

"You don't remember me, do you?" the daemon asked through his teeth. "I knew I would find you one day."

"I don't know what you're talking about." Yet that same familiarity struck me hard and fast.

The daemon leered at me before speaking. "You escaped me once before. It won't happen again."

"Who are you? What are you talking about?" He moved closer with each sidestep. I remained on guard but let him get within striking distance. Let him think he had the upper hand.

"You don't remember our time together? That hurts, little flower."

The nickname struck a chord in me. Some hidden memory struggled to surface. With a gasp, I said, "Ferghus."

"Oh, you do remember. How nice. It will make our reunion much more pleasant."

With that, he lunged. I was ready for him. Using his own strength against him, I redirected his attack and launched him over my shoulder. The move broke the spear in two. He landed hard but rolled and managed to spring back up. With a growl, he came in again, though not as direct. We moved and struck like a macabre dance. Around us, the battle waged on. Ferghus' warriors were falling. So were mine. I saw Lenna drop even as I circled Ferghus and sized up his weakness.

Lenna's daemon mate roared with fury and tore across the field to her side. I watched as he blocked a fellow daemon's attack with one arm while he ripped open a vein in the other with his teeth. He pressed the gushing wound to Lenna's mouth. She fought it at first but looked too injured to persist. I had a feeling he wrested control over their telepathic link to ensure she took his blood to heal.

This was twice that he'd protected her. Any further doubt about their relationship disappeared.

"You're losing," I spit at the daemon commander. "You might as well give up now."

He looked around, took in each individual match. He hadn't expected the people living in Mescalero to put up so much of a fight— or for his own to turn against him. His lip pulled back in a grimace. "We are not finished here. Now I know how to find you, little one. You won't get away so easily again."

With his arms outstretched, Ferghus roared to the heavens. The earth began to rumble and shake with an all-too-familiar quake. They were about to disappear. Again.

No. Not this time.

Ferghus looked at me once more and smirked. With a burst of preternatural speed, I tackled him as the ground split open to swallow him whole. I didn't manage to take him by surprise, though. He wrapped his arms around my back, his claws sinking into my ribs and up into my heart. Samson's cry of anguish echoed in my mind as the world around me turned to black.

Chapter 14

Though he had never considered himself a fighter, Samson couldn't help but see the beauty in Lani's lethal movements. She exuded grace and power, and he was filled with so much pride he was near to bursting.

She flowed from one opponent to the next, redirecting attacks and putting down daemons with the ease of a well-practiced dance.

Samson did his best to hold his own, but his human strength was no match for the hulking creatures. He brought up a sword to block against a spear, but the daemon pushed through his defense like a hot knife through butter. He hit the ground hard. On his back, Samson watched the weapon start its downward trajectory, but before it could find a home in his chest, the daemon arched back, mouth dropping open to let loose a primal shriek as he fell to his knees.

Lani stood in his place—his own personal *ángel de la vida.*

She pulled him to his feet, and they went back-to-back. Samson blocked and sliced as Lani broke another's arm. She squared off with the golden-eyed daemon as Samson spotted Chayton, in his wolf form, take a hit to his flank. He stumbled and hit the ground hard.

Samson ran before he could think. With a battle cry that would have made his ancestors proud, Samson swung the sword with everything he had. The daemon dropped to a knee, and Atienn ripped into him with his wolf's teeth. Swinging the sword in a wide arc, Samson sliced through the daemon's neck and watched with bleak satisfaction as the head rolled across the ground.

Shock rippled down the mental path Samson and Lani shared. A name shimmered in her mind even as she spoke it aloud. "Ferghus."

Samson spun to face her as the golden-eyed daemon attacked, and Lani flipped him over her shoulder. He bounced back quickly, and they circled, striking and moving faster than Samson could track. Around them, the battle continued on, but Samson couldn't look away from his mate. Even as he reached down to support Chayton in standing, even as he saw Lenna fall and another daemon leap to her side and force his blood down her throat, Samson's gaze was trained on Lani.

The tide was turning against the daemons, and the golden-eyed commander knew it. He stretched his arms wide, and Samson saw Lani's expression morph from triumphant to outraged to grim determination in an instant.

Samson watched, helpless, too slow, as his mate launched herself at the daemon with a tackle that would have wowed even the most hardcore football fans. Leaving Chayton with his twin, Samson raced for the spot where the ground had literally swallowed the daemon and Lani. He collapsed to his knees when he felt the echoing pain of claws sinking into flesh. Agony consumed him and erupted in a guttural scream that rose to the heavens.

Lani was gone.

∞ ∞ ∞

SAMSON SAT IN THE COMMUNITY center feeling like a hollowed-out shell. Everything that had happened from the moment Lani disappeared had been a blur. Those injured in the fight had been brought in and were being looked at by the healers. There seemed to be a constant flurry of activity, but Samson sat alone, the eye in the storm.

He didn't know how much time had passed. Without Lani, everything felt meaningless. Raven brought him a plate of food that sat next to his foot, untouched. His dad had checked on him but, with nothing to say, had patted his shoulder and left.

Part of him knew he should get up, help his family, check on his mom in the makeshift infirmary. Viktor and the elders would be making plans; the daemons hadn't won, but they hadn't been defeated, either, and they would be back.

Samson knew all of this, but still, he sat, knees pulled to his chest, staring at nothing, vaguely aware of people moving around him, but insubstantial, as if they existed in another reality. Their voices were muffled, their faces blurred. He couldn't focus on anything but the emptiness inside.

More time passed. The frantic air calmed, though it didn't wholly diminish. He should sleep. Eat. Help. Something.

But he couldn't.

The sun began its descent before another person attempted conversation. This time, Frances sat beside him, and from his peripherals, Samson could see Frances looked as defeated as he felt.

"Words aren't enough, but I'm sorry."

Dropping his head, Samson let out a choked sob. He hadn't cried, hadn't even really spoken since that moment he felt the claws barreling through Lani's insides. The pain of losing her consumed him, left him raw and bleeding. Frances rested a hand on Samson's shoulder, and the two shared in their grief.

Wiping his eyes with a sleeve, Samson finally looked up. His voice came out hoarse. "What's happening?"

"They're preparing for an attack."

"Tonight?"

"We don't know. Viktor's had a rotation of scouts all day. No sign of the daemons yet."

Samson's hands tightened into fists. A wild, irrational part of him wished there was a daemon before him now. He would rip and tear until nothing remained but scraps. "I will avenge her." *Or die trying.*

The unspoken alternative didn't need to be spoken aloud to be understood. Frances twisted his fingers together, staring at the tangled appendages as his story came out. "I lost my sister. She was my twin, but I was responsible for her. I went down a dark path after it happened, turned into a creature with a black soul. I still haven't forgiven myself for losing her or for letting the darkness consume me. I can't tell you not to do this because that would make me a hypocrite, but I can say it doesn't end well."

"I can't live without her."

"She would want me to protect you."

"For what? Tell me the truth, Frances. What happens to mates when one dies?"

Frances swallowed hard and fixed his gaze on something beyond the building. "When one dies, the other follows. But you're different, Samson. You haven't been converted. You can survive this."

"It doesn't matter. It feels like half of me is gone; do you understand that?"

"Yeah," Frances said with a sigh. "I understand that."

When the argument disappeared, so did Samson's ire. "I'm sorry about your sister. Thank you for trusting me, telling me, before and now—Lani wouldn't. She said it was your tale to tell."

"She was a good friend."

"So are you."

They shared a somber smile before Frances said, "We need to protect your family."

"We will." It was the last thing Samson would do. He would make sure his family was safe before joining Lani in the next life.

It was time to stop wallowing. Samson gained his feet and held out a hand for Frances before finding Viktor and the rest of the elders. Frances left him to it. "I'm going to work on more protection sachets."

Samson walked toward the office that Viktor had commandeered and glanced into an adjoining room. The sight in there made his heart ache. Lani wasn't the only victim of the daemons. Three others had died defending their home. Samson's grandmother—Santiago and Viktor's mom—had already washed the bodies in preparation for burial. The families would sit vigil through the night, barring another attack.

There was no body for Grandma Gouyan to prepare for Lani. There would be no rituals for a safe journey to the afterworld. She would be forever adrift.

When grief struck anew, Samson searched desperately for a distraction. He sought out his uncle. "Where can I help?"

"The weapons need cleaning and sharpening," Viktor said. He understood Samson's need for action. "Your dad is in there, too."

"How are the injured?"

"Coming along, thanks to your mom and the others. Every off-duty doctor and nurse volunteered to help, too." Samson nodded and turned to find his father. Before he could leave, Viktor stopped him. "I'm sorry, nephew. She is with the spirits now."

"Is she? We have no body. What if she is wandering, lost, forever?"

"Have faith, Samson. She died a warrior's death; the spirits will guide her."

It wasn't good enough. Nothing could make up for it, not even the death of that golden-eyed daemon who stole the very breath from Samson's lungs, but it was a start.

Samson found his father in the gym, which, on any other day, was filled with children's laughter as they played. This night, weapons of every variety in states from mangled to shining littered the floor while volunteers worked to revive the worst.

In the center of the gym, Santiago ran a blade against a whetstone before testing the edge with his thumb. With a nod of approval, he set the sword down and glanced up to find his son standing before him.

Without a word, Santiago handed Samson a dagger and his stone before grabbing another. They worked in silent companionship, even when Santiago could feel his son's agony in the air between them.

"You will continue to fight?"

Samson didn't look up from his work. "I will make sure our family is safe."

"We have our ways of dealing with grief."

"Cutting my hair won't bring her back."

"It's not supposed to. We keep her alive by remembering her, by honoring what she gave to the world."

"It's not enough. The connection we have, it runs deeper than I can even explain. She didn't just die; she took half of me with her."

"Believe it or not, that is the same way I feel about your mother."

Now Samson did look up. "What would you do, then? If something happened to Mom, what would you do?"

"I would grieve, and I would find a way to live. You know our ancestors stay with us. They live on in our hearts and minds and stories."

"It's not fair," Samson said, his voice quiet.

"Life's not fair, son. That's why they call it life."

"That makes no sense."

"Perhaps not. When the road is uneven, it forces us to find a new path. In struggle lies the opportunity for growth. In death lies life. Lani died for us, the same as Marco, Luis, and Dean. They are heroes. We must honor their sacrifice by living."

Samson didn't respond. How could he find meaning in this loss? How could he honor Lani's sacrifice when every breath felt like a betrayal?

He knew, deep down, that his dad was right. But at the same time, it was different for him. It was different for Elementals. He would do his duty to his people, but after that? He would join his mate.

Handing the sharpened dagger back to his dad, Samson stood. "I need some air."

Understanding in his eyes, his dad nodded once, and Samson made his escape. Outside, the sun had set, the moon just starting its journey into the sky. He walked without purpose, letting his feet carry him where they would.

Samson found himself at the spot where Lani had disappeared. The ground was undisturbed, when at the very least there should be some variation of the earth to mark the spot. He sank to his knees, fingers digging into the dirt as if he could somehow reach her through sheer force of will. "Lani," he said, voice cracking. "I'm so sorry. I should have protected you."

But there was no answer, only the soft rustle of tumbleweed skittering across the ground. He closed his eyes and automatically reached out to her with his mind, but he only found silence. A void where her dazzling presence should have been.

He didn't know how long he knelt there, lost in grief. Time seemed to lose all meaning once again. When he heard footsteps approaching, Samson looked up to see Frances a few feet away. "They're calling a meeting. Viktor wants everyone inside."

Samson nodded and pushed himself to his feet. His legs were stiff and unsteady, as if he'd aged a hundred years in the span of a few hours. Together, the two men made their way back to the community center.

Inside, the atmosphere was tense. Everyone had gathered in the main room, waiting for Viktor to speak. Samson spotted his parents standing together, along with his grandmother and other elders in chairs. Raven caught his eye from across the room, her expression concerned and somber.

Viktor stepped forward, his voice carrying over the murmurs of the crowd. "We have lost much today, but we cannot let our grief consume us. The daemons will return, and we must be ready. We will honor our fallen by fighting in their name, by protecting what they died to save."

Outside, the moon reached its apex on its final night of being full. Shouts erupted throughout the community center like a storm cloud breaking open and releasing a deluge of powerful winds and rain, echoing off the walls and reverberating through the hearts of all who heard them. Feet skidded across the floor in a desperate rush, the sound of metal scraping against metal filling the room as hands fumbled to grab weapons. Boots scuffed against the ground as more and more sprang into action.

Seconds later, alarms sounded; they were under attack.

Chapter 15

Balancing on a large stone, I closed my eyes and concentrated. Tristan had created a water dragon just that morning; I should be able to do the same. With one eye, I peeked out at the soothing flow of water, expecting to see something. But when I saw nothing had happened, I opened both eyes and let my shoulders drop.

"I'll never be as good as Tristan." Flopping down on the stone, I pushed my lip out in a pout. We were twins. Born just minutes apart. We came from the same stock. Why was he so much more powerful than me?

Our mother said I would grow into my powers. That Tristan was the anomaly, being able to do what he did. Shifting in the womb, by the goddess! Our poor mother.

It wasn't that I didn't have my talents. Even now, the birds in the trees spoke to me. As did the small creatures, tumbling over and around each other in the brush. The larger ones, too—though we didn't have many of those in New Zealand.

I felt more than heard the intrusion on my pity party. A large paw, stepping carefully through the tangle of trees. My heart beat not in fear but excitement.

Standing quickly and spinning toward shore, I sent happy, calm images toward whatever creature had come to visit. A huge head poked through the foliage, its strange golden eyes watching me with unwavering intensity.

"It's all right. I'm a friend," I said aloud, even as I continued to push the images toward the large cat. Though I couldn't see the rest of the body, I was sure it was a panther. "Have you come to visit? I love visitors."

One calculated step after another, the rest of the animal appeared. He stopped at the water's edge, his glittering golden eyes never leaving my face. I grinned, showing off my missing front tooth.

Then, the panther began to shimmer. Disappointment shot through me. Just an Elemental, come to reprimand me. What I wouldn't give to meet a real panther!

But the man that crouched on shore as he transformed from animal to human was like no other Elemental I'd ever seen. He was beautiful—I wrinkled my nose at thinking a man beautiful, but I had no other word for it. But under his beauty lay a darkness I didn't understand.

"Who are you?" I asked.

"My name is Ferghus. What is your name?"

"Lani."

"You have a wonderful gift, little flower."

His compliment made me sit straighter; his nickname made me blush. "Thank you."

"What are you doing out here, all alone?"

My shoulders dropped again. He *was* here to yell at me. "Practicing."

"Oh? What are you practicing?"

"Making a water dragon. My brother can do it; I should be able to!" His lips twitched at my defiance. So far, he hadn't yelled. Hope blossomed in my chest. "Are you friends with my parents?"

"No, little one. I'm not. But I can help you if you'd like."

"You can?" I stood now and jumped from rock to rock until I landed at his feet. I looked up—and up and up. He was so *tall*. "How?"

He knelt, and though he still towered over me, it didn't feel so strange. Pointing out at the water, Ferghus said, "Find a point in the river to look at. Just one spot. Don't follow the stream or look at more than one thing. Focus. Feel the soil beneath your feet. Picture the dragon in your mind. Ask the water to create it for you."

His hand rested against my back. I felt a strange warmth spread through my chest. Droplets of water jumped and danced, crashing together to form a small dragon. It flew up a few feet, then dipped and curved before dispersing back into the river.

Looking up at Ferghus with a grin, I saw his own smile of approval. Before I could say anything or try something new, Tristan spoke into my mind. *Lani, where are you? Mother wants us to help with gardening.*

"I have to go. Will I see you again?"

"I'll be here tomorrow, little flower. But you must do me a favor."

"Anything," I said, eyes wide and earnest.

"You must keep our practices a secret, even from your brother. He'll be jealous that you're learning more than he is, and if your parents find out, they won't allow you to visit me anymore."

"Oh, I promise, I won't say a word."

"Good. Then I'll see you tomorrow."

With a wave, I turned and ran toward home.

I MET FERGHUS IN SECRET nearly every day for years. He taught me anything I wanted to learn. Not only did I look up to him, I loved him like an uncle. There were times I asked him to meet my family or even the other children I played with. Tristan, Jared, Hugh. Jace and his brother, Jeremiah. Dante and his sister, Dezra. We'd all been born within ten years of each other, a rare occurrence for Elementals. But he always told me no, that our practice had to remain a secret.

Then, one day, everything changed.

At seventeen, I looked like an adult but was still considered young for my people. I ran with my friends: Tristan as a jaguar, Jared and Hugh as wolves, Dante as a leopard, Jace, Jeremiah, Dezra, and me on two feet.

Dezra was my closest friend, apart from Tristan. We'd learned at a young age to band together against the boys. We told each other everything, except for the one secret I couldn't share. When the sun hit the midpoint in the sky, I told Dezra I had to leave.

"What for now?" she asked with exasperation. She had long, dark hair, much like mine—but her eyes were a beautiful blue. "You're always disappearing. Stay. I hate when you leave me with the boys."

"I'll be back later. I have chores."

"You always have chores. Why doesn't Tristan?"

I shrugged. It was getting more and more difficult to evade her questions. "I just do. I'll see you later."

After I said goodbye to Tristan and the others telepathically, I went to find Ferghus. He met me as usual—our training spot had changed several times throughout the years, and we had been practicing in a cave for about a month.

I could tell something was wrong the instant I stepped foot into the cave. He paced the ground, his strange golden eyes burning with an unfamiliar fire. The darkness that had always been at bay hovered around him like a second skin.

My instincts told me to run, but I'd come to love Ferghus as a member of my family. If he battled something, I would do everything I could to help.

"What is it? What's wrong?"

"I need help, little flower."

"Anything, Ferghus. You know that. Tell me what I can do."

"You have to come with me. Away from your family, your friends."

The breath expelled from my lungs. I stepped back, shaking my head in denial. "Why would you ask that of me?"

"It's the only way. The only way to protect you."

"I can't just leave them."

"No, she can't."

I spun around, gasping at the sight of Dezra standing there, livid as could be. Ferghus growled his displeasure from behind me. "Dezra, what are you doing here?"

"Me? What are *you* doing here? With him?"

"Who are you to speak to me that way?"

Dezra straightened her spine and stared him down. My friend had always been fearless. "I am Dezra Paora, and you cannot speak to me that way. You also cannot take my friend."

Ferghus stalked forward and gripped my forearms. His eyes blazed into mine. "You must come with me. Please. After all I have done for you, this is all I ask."

"Ferghus, I—" I didn't know what to do. I didn't want to leave, but I cared for Ferghus.

His expression softened. For a moment, I could see past the darkness and into the man I'd come to know better than my own family. "Please, Lani. My little flower. I need you. Your friend can come with us."

"Don't listen to him, Lani! What are you thinking?" Dezra grabbed my upper arm, but I couldn't look away from Ferghus.

"Of course. Of course I will help you."

His face transformed again, hardened. The darkness returned. His incisors lengthened into fangs; his fingers stretched into claws. One sank into my soft flesh as the other gripped Dezra. Two long, elegant horns protruded from his head.

Our screams of terror echoed against the cave walls as the world we'd known disappeared from view.

LANI. MY LASHES STRUGGLED TO lift. The voice was unfamiliar, yet soothing. I must have screamed aloud as well as in my memory. My eyes opened, and I saw a woman I knew instinctively I could trust. "You have been gravely injured, Lani. Relax while I heal you."

"Who are you?" I asked, my voice groggy and cracked.

"My name is Reya. I'm a healer; I can help you."

"What...what happened?"

"I'm not sure. You've been injured; that's all I know."

"Ferghus." I spit the name. The woman with red-streaked hair and amber eyes looked back at me. Recognition instantly flared between my soul and hers. The woman from the vision. "I...I know you."

"And I know you, Lani."

"How?"

She smiled, gentle and calm. "We are sisters."

"I don't have a sister."

"Your brother is my mate."

"My brother...." Struggling to piece things together, I realized I lay not just on the earth but in it. Darkness surrounded us, yet I could see. And Reya—she was here, yet not here. "I remember now. Tristan."

"He has been searching for you for a long time. Our physical bodies are close, but we are unable to break through the barrier."

"Then how are you healing me?"

That gentle smile again. "I'm a spirit walker. Now, lie still, I need to finish healing you. We are lucky that he missed your heart, but there is still considerable damage."

I did as she asked; I had no reason to argue. A warmth spread through my limbs. Reya's spirit, connecting to mine, traveling through me. Worry for Samson, for his family, gnawed at me. I remembered latching onto Ferghus as we crashed through the earth, but how I got here—wherever here was—remained fuzzy.

The warmth retreated, and Reya came back into focus. "You need rest, and you'll need blood once you wake."

"I can't rest. I need to go back, to help. My mate and his family are in danger."

"You can't move right now, Lani. Please, trust me on this."

Tears sprang to my eyes. I tried to lift my hands, to wipe them away, but my limbs wouldn't cooperate. Tears were weakness. I hated showing weakness. "Please. I need to help them."

Reya looked off into the dark, her eyebrows furrowed. Whatever she'd thought of, she wasn't happy with. "There might be a way to see what's happening. We won't be able to intervene, though."

"Whatever it is, let's try it. I need to know."

Placing a palm over my heart, Reya looked deep into my eyes. "Look at me, into me. You see me. Trust me. Look at me, into me. You see me. Trust me."

Her oddly hypnotic words lulled me into a dreamlike state. Or perhaps where we'd been had been the dream. No longer able to feel the weight of my body, I drifted up, through the layers of rock and soil, trusting Reya to guide me.

We were spirit walking. Part of me wanted to freak out, but Reya kept me steady. "I know it's strange at first, but I need you to keep calm. Snapping back to your body would be...unpleasant."

I had a feeling that was an understatement. As we broke through the final layer of earth, I realized we were near the daemon settlement. We floated above the earth in our spirit forms. The sensation was at once terrifying and mesmerizing. A misty haze surrounded us—not like the horrible red haze the daemons had brought, but a dreamy mist that felt soothing and calm.

By mutual agreement, we flew closer to the camp. Without eyes, we could see the entire area at once, hear each conversation if we wished. The sensation was completely disorienting, but I didn't let that deter me. I had to know what was happening.

The entire group of daemons stood around the bonfire where they'd attempted their ritual. I recognized Kayne and Irvyn. Wynne—Lenna's mate. The others, I didn't know by name before, but the information came to me as soon as I thought it. Ferghus commanded this group, though Wynne was second. I could also feel their intent. See their spirits—or lack thereof.

"We came upon a battle between our Elemental friends and daemons—who had shadowmen with them," Reya said. "Kate is able to see auras, to heal them. But when she tried to connect to the daemons, her ability didn't work."

"They don't all have a soul."

"We didn't believe any of them did. I'm happy to see some of them might have goodness in them. They might be able to be saved."

"Those two caught me in their camp but didn't attack or send up an alarm. That one saved Lenna—a young shifter on the reservation. There is definitely goodness among them. But they didn't actively help us, either. Something held them back."

The bonfire surged with heat, shot sparks high in the sky. We felt the need to lurch back, though it couldn't harm us. The daemons watched with varying expressions, some devout, some nervous. Horns rose from the flames, one large pair protruding from high on the head and a second, shorter pair arcing from the temple, past the ears and back. Once the shoulders and chest were hovering above the flames—and well above the group of daemons—he paused. This daemon looked twice as large as the others, his rage almost palpable in the air.

He could have been handsome once. But the ravage of time and anger had turned him grotesque. On closer inspection, I realized he was missing an eye. An empty socket, long scarred over, sat in its place. He didn't bother to wear a patch.

As one, the group of daemons knelt on one knee and brought their right hand in a fist to their left shoulder. "Lord Balor."

"Rise, my warriors. Ferghus, report."

"Our full moon ritual was interrupted, my lord."

"How could you let this happen?" he screamed. In my spirit form, I winced back.

"There are Elementals here. We took one out, but one remains. Others stand at the border, attempting to breach our barrier."

"You had a simple job: get me more souls. They are humans. Weaklings. Yet you seem unable to perform such a basic task." Ferghus stood silent, his head bowed. Balor's gaze rested on each of the warriors in turn. His lip pulled back in a snarl. "There are traitors among you."

"Who, my lord?"

Balor focused back on Ferghus, his sneer still apparent. "It doesn't matter who. Perhaps you all need a reminder of what we do and why."

He snapped his fingers, and every daemon collapsed to the ground, palms pressed to the sides of their heads in agony. Anger rose up, sharp and fast. I wanted to gouge Balor's other eye out. No creature deserved to be treated this way. Especially not the ones who still fought against the evil they'd been surrounded with their entire lives.

Their torment dragged on for minutes. When he'd decided they'd had enough, Balor snapped again. Relief was instantaneous, though they were slow in getting up. "Don't make me remind you again. Now, attack the tribe. Bring me my souls."

On their feet, the daemon warriors bowed their heads and brought their fists up to their chests. "Yes, Lord Balor."

"We have to warn them. We have to help," I said to Reya. "Bring me to Samson, please."

Reya capitulated, and we drifted away from the daemon warriors preparing for another battle. Our spirit forms moved toward the community center and found the grounds quiet. I could see the guards on the lookout. They had no idea what was coming.

We were too late. The alarm went up. The daemons charged across the expanse of desert, spears raised high with a battle cry. The brave men and women of the reservation poured through the doors and stood together as a pack, a family. Trepidation rippled through me. They couldn't possibly survive this.

They braced for impact. I saw Samson there, beside his father, his uncle. Leading the charge, though his eyes were red from grief. He thought I was dead. My easy-going mate with a warrior's spirit. And there was Frances, working his magic to keep as many safe as he could. Ex-shadowman turned human protector.

The daemons moved ever closer. I fought against the restraints of my spirit form. I could see so much yet do nothing about it. Reya grunted with my struggles and spoke soothingly. "Wait. Look."

From behind the defensive group, a small figure stepped from the door. She took in the scene with the wisdom and calm of one well beyond her years. My heart—in my body, underground—lurched into my throat.

"What is she doing? She has to go back inside. She needs to stay safe." I knew Reya felt the same protective instinct, yet she did nothing. "Please. We have to help."

Kateri pushed her way through, sneaking under legs and ducking under weapons. When she got to the front, Samson and his father both tried to grab her, hold her back. Protect her.

She would have none of it. Kateri stepped forward, several steps in front of the rest. Back straight, eyes steady, hands fisted at her sides, she challenged the daemons with her stare. The ten-year-old girl no longer existed. In her place stood an ancient being, strong and powerful, commanding attention. Demanding obedience.

Kayne was the first to stop. He stood several feet away, gazing back at her. His arms flew out to his sides, halting the rest in their path. The air itself seemed to still, to hold its breath. All eyes were riveted to the unbelievable scene unfolding.

The small girl, an army at her back. The devil warriors facing them, spread out with lethal intent. Not a word was spoken. A beat of time passed; two. Still, the world remained frozen.

"I see you, Kayne of the Tuatha Dé Danann. Your soul shines brightly for me, as do several others. Stand down before more blood is shed this day." Utter silence met Kateri's request. She straightened further, stared them down. The power emanating from this girl rivaled the gods. "Stand with us, and Balor shall no longer have control over you or your lives. Your souls are not lost."

Kayne knelt and dropped his weapon to the ground. He bowed his head and murmured, "I swear my life and fidelity to you, Biroġ of the Mountain, now Kateri of the Mescalero. You have my undying loyalty."

Irvyn dropped to his knee, bowed his head. Swore his life to Kateri. As did Wynne and another I'd only come to know in this spirit form. Emrys.

Others, their souls shining brightly, hesitated in doing the same. Something stopped them from renouncing Balor. I could only imagine what that could be.

Behind Kateri, the army made up of her family and friends stared in shock. Before her, daemon warriors were on their knees with heads bowed. The daemons with no soul snarled at their cowed counterparts. I stared at Ferghus, trying to see a spark of the man I had once thought of as family. Though he had no aura like Kayne and Wynne and the others, my eyes snagged on a strange spot of golden light in the vicinity of his heart. It was impossible to focus on it, as it only appeared in my peripheral when I looked away, so I put it down to a trick of the light or this spirit form or simple wishful thinking.

Ferghus looked at his warriors in supplication and screamed for them to get back to their feet. When they didn't listen, his glare switched to the young girl still refusing to back down. With a feral growl, Ferghus thrust his spear into the sky. "Attack!"

With raised spears, his followers repeated the shout before charging. Ferghus went after Wynne first—betrayal of his second-in-command able to touch a part of him that Kateri's plea could not. I felt my heart break. The man I'd once cared for had deceived me twice. There would be no redemption for Ferghus. The still-hesitating daemons didn't help, but they didn't join the charge, either. They remained standing, clearly struggling with a decision.

Weapons clashed. Frances threw spells out but waged a losing battle as each chant was quickly counteracted by one of the daemons. Shifters howled and lunged and sank their teeth into any exposed skin.

I watched it all simultaneously, rage burning through me at my inability to help. Above it all, I watched my mate block an attack, issue one of his own. Two daemons ganged up on him, and he toppled to the ground.

Terror seized me as one of the daemons heaved his spear back and thrust it straight into Samson's heart.

Chapter 16

My eyes shot open with a gasp on my lips. Reya sat next to me, her hand against my heart, just as we'd been before our spirit trip. I sat up, relieved at the ability to perform that small action, and tried to stand.

"Wait, Lani," Reya said, gripping me with a strength that belied her small stature. Still, I struggled against her. I had to get to Samson. It couldn't be true. I couldn't have lost him now after I'd just found him. I could convert him, as Talon had done for Jade. I would save him. Reya spoke sharply to get my attention. "Lani! We have time. These things have yet to come to pass."

"What?"

"We were watching the future. The daemons are only beginning to gather now."

"I need to get out of here. I need to go to them. Please. I can't lose him."

"I know. Just give me a moment." She closed her eyes. Waiting, watching, I startled back when two tiny forms appeared in her arms. Two sets of identical eyes blinked up at me. Two familiar sets of eyes—my eyes. Tristan's eyes. I gasped as Reya smiled. "Lani, I'd like you to meet your niece and nephew."

"I'm—I'm an aunt?"

"You are. They can't wait to meet you in person. For now, they are going to help you get out of here."

"How?"

"Leia has an affinity for the earth. Nicola can boost her power and yours. Now hold tight, get ready. We wait for you at the border. Come get us, first, and we will help you defeat the daemons. It is the only way."

Sucking in a breath, I nodded. I had to think clearly. With a not-quite-steady hand, I reached out, mesmerized by my niece and nephew's tiny smiles, the intelligence shining in their eyes. Leia gripped my finger with her tiny fist, and I felt a jolt of power. The earth began to shake. Above me, a tunnel formed. As one, we floated up—Reya in her spirit form, holding her twins. Leia connecting us. I didn't know which of us made it happen or if it was a combination. But as we rose through the bowels of the earth, I saw the beauty in each layer. Roots and rocks seemed to gather at the edges of the tunnel, wanting, needing to be close to the little girl before me.

We broke through as the sun dipped low in the sky. The third night of the full moon had arrived; I must have spent a full day healing in the ground. Reya and the twins disappeared from view, their spirits returning to their bodies. I stood with renewed strength, with renewed purpose.

My family had arrived.

Samson. A wave of relief washed through me when I could feel him, our connection. Though I'd believed Reya, having it confirmed did wonders for my psyche. I could feel his intense grief and overall apprehension. On hearing my voice, happiness burst through him, smothering our connection with love. For a moment, I gathered it around myself, let it bolster me.

You're okay. Oh, Lani, thank God you're okay. His voice was thick with tears.

More than. I'll be there soon. This is going to sound strange, but I need you to trust me.

He took a moment to pull himself together. I could only imagine what it had been like for him today, not knowing my fate. Thinking me dead. *Of course. What do you need?*

The daemons are coming. Stand strong, but let Kateri through.

Kateri? What do you mean?

You'll know. Just don't hold her back. Please, trust me.

I do, Lani. With my life.

I love you, Samson. I had to tell him, just in case.

I love you, too. Come back to me soon.

With that, I began to run. Away from the daemon settlement, straight for the border. Opening myself up, I let the earth direct me to my destination. Through the thick red haze, slowing only when I felt the edge of the barrier. I kept moving forward, waiting for it to be clear enough to see beyond.

The buzz grew stronger, warning me back. I didn't listen. Edging forward in small steps, I paused only when I could finally see the other side.

Talon. His easy smile broke through, reminding me so much of Samson. He was my family—had been since the day he'd saved me from shadowmen in the woods of Wisconsin. I smiled back, then switched my gaze to Reya. She was even more stunning in real life. Her eyes shined with the love of a sister.

Finally, I looked at the intimidating man at her side. Unabashed tears fell from his dark eyes. My own shimmered with them; even without the memory of our time together fresh in my mind, I realized my soul would have recognized his.

Tristan. My brother.

On instinct, I raised my hand and placed my palm against the barrier. Tristan copied the movement, and as we pressed against each other, the barrier sparked. A loud crack sounded, and the entire thing began to waver and fizzle out.

With a whoosh of air that left us breathless, the barrier collapsed. In the deafening silence that followed, our palms touched, and I stared in shock. Power surged between us. My knees went weak, and I would have toppled to the ground, but Tristan wrapped his arms around me and crushed me to his chest.

"Lani. I can't believe it's you. I thought you were lost to me."

"Tristan." Letting the tears fall freely now, I sank into him and the moment. We didn't have long, but we both needed this. Pulling back, I wrapped Reya in a hug, then Talon. Another man stood with them, with pale hair and sky-blue eyes. He introduced himself as Aden. "I'm so happy to see you all. Where's Jade?"

"With the twins," Reya said. "I hate to rush this, but we've got somewhere to be."

"Yes," I answered, reaching out and clasping Tristan's hand. A strange power flowed between us—the strength of the twin bond. Suddenly, that part of me that had always felt empty was filled, overflowed. I was whole again. "We need to help my mate and his family."

Without further discussion, we began to run. Using our preternatural speed, we ate up the miles between us and Samson with ease. I could see the daemons halt in their tracks, just as I'd witnessed with Reya in spirit form. Kateri stood at the front of the pack, tall and straight and terrifyingly brave.

Kayne stopped, they spoke. He knelt.

And we surrounded the remaining daemons. Ferghus looked at me, and I found myself searching once again for the man that was. So quickly I might have made it up, I saw a flicker of relief on seeing me alive. Before I could be sure, his expression morphed into something akin to fear. His gaze skipped between Tristan, Reya, Aden, and Talon. His shoulders sank, knowing his defeat was imminent.

"Ferghus," I called out. "If ever you cared for me, stand down. No more blood needs to be shed this day."

He hesitated, his golden eyes latching back on me. The years of memories flooded the air between us. Then his expression shuttered. Hardened. Just like that day in the cave. The call of his master remained too strong.

Fear transformed into anger, determination. He raised his spear and called for attack. I called out a warning to Wynne, and he was able to block Ferghus' strike. Kayne, Irvyn, and Emrys gained their feet and countered the assault.

I went after the one I'd watched kill my mate. Launching onto his back, I wrapped my hands around his thick neck, lifted and turned until I heard the sickening crack. The daemon crumpled to the ground. I followed him down but landed on my feet and met Samson's gaze across the small battlefield. Shock and concern crossed his face, and for a moment, I worried his love would diminish from seeing me kill with such brutality.

I shouldn't have. Quickly recovering, Samson pointed and spoke into my mind. *Behind you!*

Spinning, I ducked under a spear and swiped at the daemon's belly with a clawed hand. From my peripheral, I watched as Tristan moved through enemy ranks with stunning ease. The tribe had joined the fray, much as I'd seen in Reya's vision.

Kateri looked to the right and left, her dark, ageless eyes taking in the whole scene with disgust. Despite their best efforts, the small army of Gifted was being pushed back and overrun. Viktor blocked an attack but got a spear swipe along his upper arm from another.

A guttural, ethereal scream tore through the night. Stunned for the briefest of moments, all movement stopped. Filled with a rage that frightened even the most fearsome warrior, Kateri lifted her child's foot and stomped the ground. Great cracks shot through the earth, expanding out from her contact. We all stared as the ground opened and swallowed our aggressors whole.

Deafening silence settled over the land as soon as the earth closed again. Frozen for a beat, then two, I finally snapped out of it, ran to my mate, and kissed him hard. He lifted me off my feet and spun me around. I took this moment, too. We'd earned it.

I could hear Reya ordering people around. There were injured that needed to be tended to. Pulling back and taking Samson's hand, I faced all those around us. My family, his. The four daemons who had sworn loyalty to Kateri.

Everyone looked shell-shocked, not just from the brief but intense battle with daemons but at what Kateri had done. When I looked at the young girl, her eyes met mine with a wisdom beyond her years. Then she blinked, and whatever had taken over her disappeared. She sank to the ground.

Kayne rushed to her, but the look on Viktor's face as he stepped aggressively forward made the daemon pause. Viktor knelt to his daughter and scooped her into his arms. The one that had been bleeding already had a makeshift tourniquet tied around it. When he stood, he faced his people. "Our battle is won, but we have much to discuss. Please go back inside. My daughter needs to be seen to, and then I will join you."

He looked over at me and gave me a nod. I understood what he asked. As Reya directed Aden and Talon to help in carrying the wounded inside, I stepped in front of the gathered daemons. With Samson on one side and Tristan on the other, I extended a hand. "Thank you for your assistance, Kayne."

He took my hand, shook it. "I should be thanking you. We've been struggling against Balor a long time. He had control over us that couldn't be broken. Until—"

"Until Kateri. She's a reincarnation of one of the original Tuatha Dé Danann, isn't she?"

"Yes. We all recognized her," he said, gesturing toward the other three who stood with him. "We thought all who opposed Balor had been defeated. Perhaps we should have known they'd find a way to return and fight."

Irvyn stepped forward and bowed his head respectfully. "We are now committed to Kateri, and we can do her no harm. But others will try. Balor will not take this defeat gracefully."

"I'm hoping you'll all be able to help us with that. We saw the maps. There are other places they're going to try to recruit, aren't there?"

"Yes, though it won't be immediate," Irvyn answered. "This will be a devastating blow to Balor. Time also flows differently in our world. They will recuperate and come back hard."

"We will be ready," Tristan assured him.

"There is another matter. I have a mate in our world. We've kept our relationships secret for fear of what Balor would do if he found out or if something like this happened. I need to smuggle her out of Murias."

I nodded and offered a reassuring smile. "So, you do have mates. I understand completely. There's nothing I wouldn't do for mine."

"Or I," Tristan said.

"We will help in any way we can," I said. "Is that why some of the others refused to swear loyalty to Kateri? I could see they wanted to."

Irvyn nodded. "Not all kept their relationships secret. Once they are able to secure their mates' safeties, we can count on them to renounce Balor and his evil."

Sneaking a glance at Kayne, I noticed his focus was on the community center at my back. Concerned for Kateri, I'd imagine. "They'll all need time, but she's in good hands."

He nodded, his jaw set. "She is still a child, though she has the wisdom of the ages buried inside. I will do nothing untoward."

"I would like to meet with the four of you and the elders once all the injured are looked after. We will have much more to discuss," Tristan said. "But right now, I would very much like to officially meet my sister's mate."

With joy about bursting from my chest, I introduced Samson to Tristan. Talon joined us, and when Samson and Talon shook hands, I could see an understanding pass between them. A family connection. "You are a descendant of Silver Moon."

"Your aunt," Samson said. "Lani made the connection."

When Talon looked at me with a question in his eye, I explained, "There is a sacred cave. I had hoped to bring you there, but it seemed to be destroyed when the barrier went up."

"Sacred things have a way of enduring," Talon said. "When everything else is figured out, I would love to visit with you."

"Would you like to come inside now? Officially meet your family?" Samson asked.

"I will stay out here for now."

Talon and I will keep an eye on this group until Reya needs me. I know you want to check on everyone inside, Tristan spoke into my mind. The familiarity of it felt comforting, if a little rusty. *You also need blood.*

The last was an observation and an offer. *Thank you. I will replenish soon; let's get everyone settled first.*

I cannot tell you how happy I am to have found you. You have become the strong, powerful woman I always knew you to be.

I didn't remember you. If I had, I would have found you sooner. Tristan—there's much I have to tell you. I remember it all.

We can speak of it later. It's the past, now. All things happen as they must. You have found your mate because of it. He seems like a good man, but I may still need to have a heart-to-heart with him.

Don't you dare, I said with a laugh. *Reya is amazing as well. I can't wait to meet your children.*

She has brought light to my life. We have much to catch up on, and we will soon. Jade will bring the twins as soon as we know it's safe.

Knowing Jade, she's chomping at the bit to be in the fray.

True, but she was the best choice to watch over the children. Even she agreed with that.

Excusing us from the daemons, I squeezed Samson's hand and brought him inside. Santiago was organizing crews to get the power back on and to assess damages. Many homes would need to be rebuilt, food replenished.

But thanks to the incredible group effort of everyone living here, few lives had been lost. As I took in the relieved faces of all those around me, I felt proud not only of them but of being part of their family.

Chapter 17

Several hours after the battle, we gathered in the small house Frances and I had rented. Tristan and Talon seemed almost too big for the space, but they settled in kitchen chairs while Reya sank into one of the more comfortable living room seats. Samson sat in the other, me on his lap. Frances stood awkwardly against the wall, Aden beside him. Though he'd come into his own during this crisis, Frances seemed to fall back to old patterns with these new Elementals around.

When we heard the knock on the door, I jumped up and threw it open. There stood Jade, her golden hair shining in the sun, her emerald eyes sparkling with happiness. "Lani!'

"Jade, I'm so happy to see you," I said, reaching out to give her a hug. With a baby on each hip, the move was awkward at best. Stepping back, I bent to greet my nephew. He squeezed my finger and giggled. When I said hello to my niece, she held both hands out for me to take her. "They're even more precious in real life."

I got a confused look from Samson at my statement but just shook my head. We'd fill each other all in later. Reya came over and shifted Nicolai from Jade's hip to hers. "Lani, I'd like to officially introduce you to Nicola, named for my father. And this is Leilani Rose."

More tears clogged my throat. I looked first at Reya, then over to Tristan. "You named her for me?"

"We did. Before Reya had a vision of you, I thought you lost to me. I wanted our daughter to at least carry a piece of you."

"That's so amazing. Thank you."

Samson came over and cooed at the young Leilani. "Leilani Rose, huh?"

Laughter bubbled out. "Is it strange for you? Falling in love with someone without even knowing their name?"

"Not at all. But I will say it's nice to meet you, Leilani Rose Amiri." He placed a gentle kiss on the baby's forehead, then one on my lips. "Two beauties."

Jade had moved to greet Frances, who looked a bit more comfortable in her presence. She then perched on Talon's lap and said, "All right, fill me in on what I missed."

We spent the next couple of hours catching up. I talked about the cave and the vision I saw in the Divining Pool. Reya told me she'd had the same vision.

Jade filled us in on the daemon battle in California and the twenty-six shadowmen that had been saved. It seemed the attack on Mescalero had happened almost immediately after that; attempting to replenish their numbers made the most sense.

Nicola bounced in his father's legs while Leia slept peacefully in Aden's arms. The twins were loved by all and constantly got shifted from lap to lap. Leia seemed to have a special connection with Aden, and I made a note to myself to ask Tristan or Reya about that later.

Finally, I told everyone about my returned memories. My time with Ferghus and how I managed to escape. "He held me on the outskirts of a daemon city."

"A daemon city? That sounds ominous. Why have we never found it?" Jade asked.

"It's not in this world," I said. "How to explain?"

"Are you saying there's a multiverse?" Samson asked.

I shook my head, but it was Jade who answered. "The otherworld. Mag Mell, the city of the fae. It's in Irish folklore."

"And what of Dezra?" Tristan asked before we got too far into mythology.

"I have no idea where he kept Dezra—if she was even there. I never saw her again after that day in the cave."

"Dante retreated into himself when the two of you went missing. He disappeared not long after, and none of us have been in contact in many years. Between Jared, Hugh, and the two of us, we'll find him and tell him what we now know. If his sister is still out there—or a captive of the daemons—”

“Perhaps Kayne or one of the others can give us more insight,” I said, hope cutting through my insides like a knife. To see my friend again, after all these years. After a moment, I continued with my story. “I was deep, deep in the earth. I fought against him a long time but finally realized I would have to play along and gain his trust. So, I did. For many years, I think. It was difficult to judge time there. I believe he truly cared for me, as much as one without a soul is capable. I used that to convince him to take me along on one of his missions.

“I didn’t know what he was doing; he wouldn’t tell me. But he took me with him on a solo mission. I finally got to breathe fresh air, see the sky. Even though it was night, I remember thinking how bright it was compared with where I’d been.

“I’d soaked up everything he’d been willing to teach me. I practiced when I was left on my own and came up with a plan; I just had to wait for my moment. When it came, I attacked. Ferghus never saw it coming. I injured him—thought I killed him. Turns out that I didn’t.

“From there, I ran. I didn’t stop until exhaustion nearly overtook me. Then, I placed a spell on myself—one that hid me from Ferghus in case he’d managed to survive. The problem was, it hid me from myself, as well.”

“I remember that day,” Tristan said quietly, rubbing the palm of his hand absently over his chest. “I could feel you. It was the first hope I'd had in many years. Nineteen years and forty-six days, to be exact. That's how long you were gone." There were several expletives muttered among the group. The truth hit me hard, as well. "I couldn't reach you through our telepathic link, but I knew you were alive. It gave me hope, at least for a brief time. When our connection severed again, it was like losing you all over."

"I'm so sorry," I murmured, reaching out to clasp his hand with mine. "I didn't expect to lose my own memories in the process. I would have come to find you."

"I don't blame you, Lani. I blame myself."

"No, don't do that, either. Guilt will do nothing to change the past, and it will only hurt our relationship now." He nodded, though his eyes remained clouded. I knew I had to change the subject. "These memories all came back to me when I tackled Ferghus and followed him into the ground. We got separated somehow, and that's when Reya came to heal me. Just before the final battle."

"I have to say, though I trusted your judgment, watching my little cousin face thirty angry daemons just about did me in," Samson said, understanding my need to move on from my lost years.

"Reya and I saw it unfold. She might have to explain exactly how that worked, as I'm still not sure." The memory of watching Samson die came unhindered to my mind, making me shudder. Samson tightened his hold on me.

What's wrong?

Something in Reya's vision. It doesn't matter now. It didn't happen. He didn't fully buy it, but he didn't press, either. There had been enough revelations for the day.

"I'm a spirit walker, as was my mother. A talent I used without my knowledge." Reya shared a loving look with her mate. "It's how Tristan and I met. My spirit traveled to his, though I didn't remember my dreams until I found him in person. I've been practicing, which is how I was able to bring you with me."

"You're a spirit walker and also a healer?"

"And a seer." She took a deep breath, let it out. "My father was a seer. Apparently, male foreseers pass their gift onto their child—and the child inherits the gifts of both parents. Plus, I have my own, the healing."

"Wow," was all I could think to say. "So, we spirit walked...into the future?"

"Basically. I pulled you into a lucid vision."

"And when you brought the twins in?"

"They are of me, so we are and always will be connected."

"This is all incredible," Samson said. "We have our own stories; I've heard them since I can remember. They seemed fantastical enough, but this?"

"We're all blown away by Reya's abilities," Jade said with a grin. "But I'd like to steer back to this other realm that apparently has daemon cities. My grandmother told me the stories of the Tuatha Dé

Danann when I was young. Balor, King of the Fomorians, the daemons. A terrible man. Said to have one large eye that could wreak destruction when uncovered. He supposedly always kept layers of cloth over it, otherwise he'd accidentally burn people up.

"He was told by a seer that his own grandson would be his downfall, so he locked his daughter in a tower so she wouldn't get knocked up. I'm paraphrasing, of course, but that's the gist of it. Well, a man got in the tower anyway and fell in love with the daughter. She had triplets, and Balor ordered them killed. Two were drowned, one survived. Lugh, the sun god. It is said he defeated Balor by striking a spear through his one eye."

"Balor was missing an eye," I said. "But it wasn't giant, and he still had one good one."

"That's the trouble with fables," Jade said with a shrug. "Passed down over generations, the stories change and details either become fuzzy or wildly inaccurate. The truth is in there somewhere, though."

"The legend of our twins also involves daemons," Samson said. "It is how they were defeated."

"What happened to Lugh?"

"Killed, eventually. But seeing as Balor isn't dead, you never really know, do you?"

"He was defeated, though," Reya said. "We're only seeing a resurgence now."

"Not exactly," Frances said. All eyes turned to him. "Irvyn told you time flows differently in their world, right? And Lani, you felt the same. Well, they're patient, for one. How long have shadowmen existed?"

"My first encounter happened not long after I escaped Ferghus," I said.

"I only came into contact with them recently, when they attacked Lani and Jade," Talon added.

"Same for me," Tristan said. "Only recently."

"My sister was taken by them," Aden said quietly. My heart went out to the man. "They almost killed me."

"I'm sorry for that," Frances said. "But do you see my point? Balor sends his slaves out, starts converting Elementals, turns them to the darkness. Most shadowmen probably don't even realize they're being turned or used. They created an army without anyone knowing. The shadowmen stayed away from threats—usually male Elementals, at least those that couldn't be turned—but they...we...still craved the light. A mate. Which is why Lani came across them more often, and why—again, I'm so sorry—why they took your sister."

We all digested that theory carefully. I spoke first. "It makes sense."

"So, the group we came across in California? That was them, what, making their move?" Jade asked.

"It seems so." Frances shrugged. "I never dealt with daemons as a shadowman. That was all my own doing."

Jade reached out and laid a palm against his arm. The tension visibly drained from Frances. "You're on the right track now."

"We need to gather all the Elementals we can find. Warn them of what's happening," Tristan said. He'd been quiet during most of the conversation, taking it all in. But when he spoke, everyone listened.

"I have an idea for that," Jade said with a grin. She looked back at Talon and kissed him on the cheek. He nodded in encouragement. "It's about time we tie the knot. We'll need a few months to plan, but I'd like to invite all Elementals we've met to our wedding."

"I love that idea," Reya said. "Gives us all a reason to meet and will give hope to those without."

"You don't think we should gather sooner?" Tristan asked.

"We'll spread the word in the meantime, but it will also take time to find and reach out to solitary Elementals."

"When are you thinking?" I asked Jade.

"October. Autumn in Wisconsin is absolutely gorgeous."

We all exchanged looks, nodded. "October it is."

Epilogue

It took a few weeks, but with the help of the gathered Elementals and the newly loyal daemons, Mescalero was put back to rights. Houses were repaired or rebuilt—thanks to not only the monetary donations from Tristan and Talon but their hard labor, as well.

Talon seemed to be in his element between getting to know his extended family and using his hands to create and repair. He showed all those willing and able how to install plumbing, electrical. How to build walls and place flooring.

Even the daemons chipped in. After the three nights of the full moon, their horns retracted, and they blended in a bit better, though their hulking forms were difficult to ignore. There was a healthy amount of fear and distrust between the tribe and the daemons. Santiago did his best to minimize that damage with his special gift, but all remained wary.

So did I, but they'd agreed to help put the reservation back to rights. In our downtime, we discussed infiltrating their home world, and the more we got to know the four individuals willing to go against everything they'd ever known, the more we began to trust them.

"We lived in what the Irish refer to as Mag Mell, in the mists of the Otherworld," Kayne explained to us one of the first evenings. Jade had given the rest of us a satisfied smirk at his confirmation. "Mag Mell used to be a beautiful, peaceful place. After Balor was defeated by Lugh, he retreated into the bowels of the earth and refused to leave. Some say he is chained there, but none know for certain. He plotted and planned his revenge, forced us all to do his bidding. His castle was built around him, and then an entire city. We call it Murias, after the Tuatha Dé Danann's original home in this world."

"Murias is a dark and dangerous place," Irvyn said, clearly the most distraught of the group. It was difficult for him, knowing his mate remained in danger. "Shea works in the kitchens of the palace. As long as she keeps her head down, she will be fine."

"We'll get her," Jade said, placing her hand over his. She took on some of his worry, relieved him of some of his stress so he could think and plan with a clear mind. "I have to say, it's pretty amazing to hear all the stories my grandma told me as a kid are actually true."

"True enough, anyway," Kayne said.

"Why do you think you four, for example, have a soul, while others—like Ferghus—don't?" Reya asked.

"Before the Tuatha Dé Danann arrived in Ireland, Balor was the king of the Fomorians. They plundered and pillaged wherever they wished. They traveled by sea or under it. That's where the name comes from—Old Irish, fo muire, means 'under the sea.' When Balor and his Fomorians arrived in Ireland, they decided to stay. He could sense the entrance to Mag Mell, known as the Land of the Ever Young. He'd been searching for a way to enter, to rule the mystical land. He staked his claim in Ireland. Then, the Tuatha Dé Danann arrived.

"For many years, the Fomorians and the Tuatha Dé Danann intermingled. Married, produced offspring. I am one such individual, as are Irvyn, Wynne, and Emrys."

"You believe you have souls because of your Tuatha Dé Danann roots?" Reya asked.

"And those that come strictly from Fomorians—such as Ferghus—do not. It also makes them more loyal to Balor."

Reya shook her head. "I have a hard time believing an entire species is wholly evil."

For a while, we all processed that. Then I asked, "Can you tell us more about Kateri? Who was she in a past life?"

For now, it was just the daemons and the Elementals gathered—this would have been a touchy subject with Viktor involved. I would figure out a good way to explain it to him later.

"Kateri is a reincarnation of Biroġ of the Mountain," Kayne answered. "Something you need to understand about Balor—he is very patient, cold, calculating. He didn't attack the Tuatha Dé Danann at first; he encouraged the intermingling. He had control over every child of Fomori, including ones that were only half. The Tuatha Dé Danann didn't realize this until it was too late.

"Even Balor took a wife and produced an offspring, thinking this would secure his position as leader. But then he was given the prophecy that his own grandson would be his downfall. He locked his only daughter, Ethniu, in a tower where she could never give birth.

"Of course, you know she did. Biroġ was a high priestess fighting against Balor's reign. She snuck Cian—Ethniu's true mate— into the tower, dressed as a woman to get past the guards. They only spent one night together, but she became pregnant and had triplet sons."

"Two were killed; one survived," Jade murmured. "Lugh."

"He was rescued, again, by Biroġ. After scooping the infant out of the lake that he was supposed to drown in, she brought him to his father to be raised. Cian, in turn, entrusted him to his brother. Balor had Cian killed for the betrayal." Kayne quieted, then looked to his fellow daemons. They seemed to come to some kind of silent, mutual agreement. Of course, I knew Kayne had the ability to speak into other's minds, so their agreement may not have been completely silent. "Biroġ did more than bring Cian to Ethniu and rescue Lugh. As a high priestess, she had powers even we know nothing about, but one we did know was that she was a foreseer. She knew Lugh would defeat Balor, but that it wouldn't be the end of his destructive reign. So, she gifted certain humans some of her abilities in every corner of the world. This gave birth to a new species."

"Elementals," I whispered in awe.

"She knew, one day, Balor would rise again. Only an army of powerful creatures had a fighting chance to defeat him, once and for all."

"When do you think we should try to enter Murias?" I asked.

The four daemons exchanged looks. They'd obviously already discussed this. "Samhain. The night the veil between the worlds is thinned."

"We must be stealthy now that we've renounced Balor," Emrys continued. "The entrance in Ireland will be our best bet."

"I always wanted to honeymoon there," Jade said with a grin. "We can put together a team while everyone is in Wisconsin for the wedding."

Having inside information of the daemons was invaluable. We spent every evening like that. I still worked for Manny during the day, though I gave my notice not long after the battle on the promise that I would train in the next person. Luckily, I had the perfect person in mind—Lenna.

She recovered in just a few days, though she remained wary of Wynne. I didn't blame her. I knew—and I believed she did, deep down—that Wynne was her mate. It couldn't be an easy thing to come to terms with.

Wynne, for his part, retained distance from Lenna. The first time I saw him interact with her was her first full day of work. I'd been showing her the accounting software when the door to the little trailer opened, and Wynne ducked inside. He had to slouch in order to stand upright, and between that fact and watching Dave's eyes grow wider the longer Wynne stood there, Lenna and I couldn't control our giggles.

He'd pulled his long, thick hair into a tail. He had retained the lighter features of the Tuatha Dé Danann, with sandy hair and deep blue eyes. In his fist, Wynne clutched a happy bouquet of sunflowers, which he thrust toward Lenna with little finesse. "These are for you. Congratulations on your new job."

"Thank you," she replied as a light blush settled in her cheeks.

"I was wondering if—I mean, I would like to—er, would you have lunch with me?"

A flustered daemon. Wonders never ceased. Lenna looked just as shocked and unable to form a cohesive answer. I decided to nudge her along. "We'll be wrapped up here in about half an hour, then she has an hour for lunch."

Lenna nodded, and Wynne sent me a grateful look. "I will come back in half an hour's time."

He bowed, then ducked back outside. Dave dragged his wide eyes from the door to us. "Who the hell was that?"

"Apparently, my lunch date," Lenna said, her breath hitching on the word date. "Oh God, do I look okay?"

"Honey, you could wear a potato sack, and that man wouldn't care."

Lenna released a slightly hysterical laugh while Dave still attempted to recover. Then, with narrowed eyes, he asked, "Is he looking for a job? I bet he could do twice the work of anyone else on our crew."

At the thought, the rest of the nerves drained from Lenna. To herself, she whispered, "Wynne in a tool belt. Hmm...."

∞ ∞ ∞

ONLY WHEN EVERY SINGLE FAMILY settled back into their own homes did we decide to broach the subject of visiting the cave.

We met with Viktor and the other elders—and Gifted—in the tribe. The first subject we raised was whether to leave all memories of the daemon attack with the non-Gifted or to make them hazy. After much debate, we decided to leave everyone on the reservation with their memories intact. I could tell Tristan wasn't happy with that result, but he respected Viktor's wishes.

Everyone involved in the attack had been willing and able to defend their land, their people. We couldn't take that away from them. The subject of visiting the sacred cave was a much less heated discussion.

"I've been out there," Viktor said. "I have not been allowed entrance yet, but I believe the earth is somehow healing itself, putting the cave to rights. Either it needs more time, or it is waiting for us all to go together. I would be happy to escort you out there."

"Thank you," Talon said. "If we are not allowed entrance, we will respect that."

"I know you will. Let's wait until dusk, as the full moon rises. The first since the daemon attack. That feels right."

"I agree," Talon said.

That night, we met together as a group. Tristan, Reya, and Aden decided to stay back with the twins, even though they had been invited. Tristan felt it was best for those with blood ties—and their mates—to go.

Viktor, Talon, Jade, Samson, and I made the trek at dusk. We stood in front of the cliff face and waited for Viktor to do the honors. He stepped forward and placed his palms against the wall. As before, it shimmered and revealed a long tunnel. When he stepped through, Samson motioned for Talon and Jade to go first. We followed, happy to find everything in place.

The paintings that I'd watch crumble with the quake were back on the wall, the Divining Pool shimmering with its mystical waters. Talon walked along the wall, skimming his hand a few inches away as I had done. When he came to the painting of his mother and aunt, I saw tears well in his eyes.

"She's very beautiful," Jade murmured.

Talon nodded and squeezed her hand. "It means the world to me that our people remember her."

"Without the past, one cannot know their future," Viktor said.

Talon reached the end of the paintings and turned to look at the well. He approached it slowly, and I watched as a strange glow began to surround him. Light at first, barely visible to the human eye. It grew wider and brighter the closer he got. Jade stayed back, recognizing he needed to do this on his own.

Reaching the edge, he looked down into the perfectly still waters. We could all see as they began to tremble. A light exploded from the well, bathing the entire cave in its warm glow.

A figure formed above the well, made of the light itself. Her arms raised above her head as if she'd dived upward through the waters and came to land before us. She floated gracefully down to the ground, her ethereal gaze on Talon.

"Mother," he gasped with tears in his eyes.

She smiled gently and reached out to cup his cheek. "My dear, sweet Talon. And this must be your mate."

Talon held out a hand for Jade and brought her to his side. Jade stared in awe at the glowing figure. "Nice to meet you."

"It brings me so much happiness to see my son with his mate." Eagle Eye looked at Viktor, then Samson and me. "My sister's descendants are as strong and resilient as I always hoped. You will have more trials ahead, but I have faith you will come through them all."

"What trials, Mother?"

"The daemons are not done. Your people will gather to celebrate your love. Alliances will be made. But the daemons are crouched in the darkness, waiting to attack. You must first rescue their puppets, take them away from their grasp."

"The shadowmen?"

Eagle Eye inclined her head. "Once that task is complete, new challenges will arise. You must all face them together."

"We will."

"I have other news." She turned to Viktor. "The twins must be found."

"The original twins? They're still alive?"

"They have been asleep for many years, waiting for the right time. There are three who have the power to wake them. Your Kai is one."

Viktor looked staggered by the news. "She is so young."

"She has time. As do the rest of your girls, but their power will not be contained."

Viktor nodded, his eyes shining. He'd been so overprotective of Kateri, especially, since the attack. Not only did she seem to be a reincarnation of a powerful being, but a daemon had his sights set on her.

I couldn't imagine doing anything different in his shoes.

"I must go," Eagle Eye continued. "I can be at peace now, having seen you again, my sweet Talon. Be happy, son, as you and your mate begin this next phase of your lives. Know that I'm always with you."

She placed her palm against his cheek once more. Talon held her there, tears flowing freely now. The light went blindingly bright for a brief moment before rushing back into the Divining Pool.

We all stared in stunned silence. Jade comforted Talon, taking on some of his heartache for her own. I held tightly to Samson's hand as Viktor wept silently.

"What do we do now?" Samson asked.

"We do as she asked," Talon said.

Viktor straightened. "We do. We make sure you two get married, and we gather our allies together. We prepare my precious children for their destinies."

"We have time," I said. "Your children have time to be children yet."

Viktor met my gaze, his hardened to his tears. "Kai already feels her calling. She hides it, but I know it. Kateri stopped being just a child the moment she stepped foot on a battleground."

"Then we do everything in our power to protect them until this threat has passed," I said firmly, sensing Samson's resolve and total agreement. "We offer the option to all Gifted to be converted into Elementals. We celebrate love by going to Jade and Talon's wedding.

"And when the time comes, we fight."

Dear Reader,

Thank you for reading *Reservation: Book Five of The Gifted Series.* I hope you enjoyed this fifth installment in The Gifted series and join us in meeting the next mated pair, Arie and Emerson, in their book, Shadowed Soul.

Though each of these books follows a different couple, not to worry—all of your favorite couples will return.

As always, you can keep up-to-date by following me on Facebook, Instagram, or TikTok @anabannovels – or visit my website, www.AnaBanNovels.com

Happy Reading!

Always,

Ana

Other books by Ana Ban

www.anabannovels.com

The Parker Grey Series

Young Adult/Crime Novels recommended for ages 13+

Abstraction; A Parker Grey Novel (Book 1)

Backfire; A Parker Grey Novel (Book 2)

Coercion; A Parker Grey Novel (Book 3)

Deception; A Parker Grey Novel (Book 4)

Dubious Endeavors; A Parker Grey Novella (Book 5)

Exposed; A Parker Grey Novel (Book 6)

Firestarter; A Parker Grey Novel (Book 7)

The Gifted Series

Fantasy Romance Novels recommended for ages 18+

Allure of Home: Book 1 of The Gifted Series

Immaculate: Book 2 of The Gifted Series

Night Shift: Book 3 of The Gifted Series

Stow Away: Book 4 of The Gifted Series

Reservation: Book 5 of The Gifted Series

Shadowed Soul: Book 6 of The Gifted Series

Vows at Dusk: Book 7 of The Gifted Series (with bonus novella, *After Dusk*)

Dark Omens: Book 8 of The Gifted Series

By the Light of the Moon: Book 9 of The Gifted Series

Seeking Redemption: Book 10 of The Gifted Series

Shelter of Smoke: Book 11 of The Gifted Series

Tangled Threads: Book 12 of The Gifted Series

Beyond the Veil: Book 13 of The Gifted Series

Clash at Midnight: Book 14 of The Gifted Series (with bonus novella, *After Midnight*)

Legacy: Book 15 of The Gifted Series

Catching Shadows

Crime/Police Procedural Novel recommended for ages 18+

The Strangers Saga

Murder Mystery Romance Novels recommended for ages 18+

Baton Rouge: Book One

Baton Rouge: Book Two

Baton Rouge: Book Three

Baton Rouge: Book Four

Baton Rouge: Book Five